Lord Nathaniel Lindsay, heir to the earldom of St Auburn.

She could not believe it—could not quite take in that her dangerous rescuer in Nay with his scarred body and quick reflexes was now a dandified Lord, known across all of England for his wealth and his power, his family lineage stretching back across the centuries.

Away from the stares she was feeling a lot better. His coat was warm, and her shivers were lessened by the touch of wool. She could smell him too, here in the carriage, the depth of him and the strength, and if her sister had not been right there beside her she might have breathed in further, allowing the colours of his beauty to explode inside, tantalising and teasing.

The scent of a man who could ruin her.

AUTHOR NOTE

SCARS OF BETRAYAL is the third book in a series about three friends: Nathaniel Lindsay, Lucas Clairmont and Stephen Hawkhurst.

The themes of family, protection and betrayal have been features of all three stories: SCARS OF BETRAYAL, MISTLETOE MAGIC and MISTRESS AT MIDNIGHT.

I hope you enjoy Cassandra and Nathaniel's story.

SCARS OF
BETRAYAL

Sophia James

Published in Great Britain 2014
by Mills & Boon, an imprint of Harlequin (UK) Limited,
Eton House, 18-24 Paradise Road, Richmond, Surrey, TW9 1SR

© 2014 Sophia James

ISBN: 978 0 263 90961 6

Harlequin (UK) Limited's policy is to use papers that are natural, renewable and recyclable products and made from wood grown in sustainable forests. The logging and manufacturing processes conform to the legal environmental regulations of the country of origin.

Printed and bound in Spain
by Blackprint CPI, Barcelona

Sophia James lives in Chelsea Bay, on Auckland, New Zealand's North Shore, with her husband who is an artist. She has a degree in English and History from Auckland University and believes her love of writing was formed by reading Georgette Heyer in the holidays at her grandmother's house.

Sophia enjoys getting feedback at www.sophiajames.net

Previous novels by the same author:

FALLEN ANGEL
ASHBLANE'S LADY
HIGH SEAS TO HIGH SOCIETY
MASQUERADING MISTRESS
KNIGHT OF GRACE
   (published as THE BORDER LORD in North America)
MISTLETOE MAGIC
   (part of *Christmas Betrothals)*
ONE UNASHAMED NIGHT
ONE ILLICIT NIGHT
CHRISTMAS AT BELHAVEN CASTLE
   (part of *Gift-Wrapped Governesses*)
LADY WITH THE DEVIL'S SCAR
THE DISSOLUTE DUKE
MISTRESS AT MIDNIGHT

Chapter One

London—June 1851

It was Nathanael Colbert walking down the wide staircase of the de Clare ballroom.

Cassandra Northrup knew it was him.

Knew it from the bottom of a rising horror and an unmitigated relief.

The same strength and height, the same dark hair, shorter now but every bit as black. She could barely take a breath, the guilt and the anger that had been stored inside and hidden for so long seeping out, winding her with its intensity.

Lord Hawkhurst, the heir to the Atherton fortune, descended beside Colbert, laughing at something Colbert had said. Disbelief made Cassie dizzy. Why would he be here in such company and dressed like an English lord? Nothing quite made sense, the wrongness of it all inviting disarray.

Shaky fingers closed around the small pottery shard that she always wore around her neck, the heavy beat of blood in her ears making her feel sick. What could this mean for her?

Carefully, Cassie opened her fan so that it covered most of her face and turned from the trajectory the pair were taking. She had to leave before he saw her. She had to escape, but that was becoming harder as shock numbed reality. Maureen clasped her hand and she was grateful for the anchor.

'You look pale, Cassandra. Are you feeling sound?'

'Perfectly.' Even her sister did not know the exact details of what had happened in the south of France all those years ago, for she had never told another soul. A private torment, the details locked in shame.

'Well, you do not look it.'

The will to survive was flowing back, the initial jolt of shock receding under reason. She doubted Colbert would recognise her at a quick glance and resolved to leave as soon as she was able to without inciting future question.

Future. The very word made her stiffen. Could she have a future if he saw her? She felt as if she stood in the ballroom in nothing but the clothes he had once found her in, the events from almost four years ago searing into memory, all anger and fear and regret.

No. She was stronger than this. In a moment she would walk farther away, into the throng of people, carefully and quietly so as to draw no attention towards herself. She had become adept at the art of camouflage within society, the skill of obscurity in a crowd almost second nature to her now. It was how she had survived, washed back into the world she had not thought to be part of again, with its strict observance of manner and rule.

Cassie's gown mirrored her anonymity, the plain dove-grey unremarkable. All around the well-heeled young ladies bloomed like flowers, in yellows and pinks and light blue, tucks, ruffs, frills and flounces adorning their bodices, sleeves and hems. Her widow's weeds were another way to hide in full view from the notice of others.

As five seconds went past, and then ten, she started to feel safer, beguiled by the noise and movement of the very large crowd.

Everything is all right...it is still all right.

Her eyes scanned the room, but Colbert was nowhere to be seen. 'I should not have come, Reena,' she said, turning to her sister. 'You manage these things with far more acumen than I. It is simply a waste of my time to be here.'

Maureen laughed. 'I hate these functions, too, but Mr Riley was adamant about the invitation being for the both of us, Cassie, and his purse is a generous one.'

'Well, as he did not show himself I doubt he would have known if I had stayed away.' She needed to leave, needed to walk towards the door as though she did not have a care in the world. The ache inside intensified.

Once she had loved Nathanael Colbert, right from the bottom of her broken life.

The thought of what had happened next made her swallow, but she shook it gone. Not here, not now. Fixing a smile on her face, she listened to Maureen ramble on about the beauty of the room and the dresses and the lines of the small shaped trees set up near the band to give the appearance of a natural grotto. A fantasy world where anything was possible, a kinder world away from all that was sordid and base and unclean. All about her happy banter tinkled, the easy discourse of people with few worries in life apart from what they would be wearing to the next social occasion or the generous inheritances they had garnered from the latest deceased relative.

A strange sound above caught her attention. Looking up, Cassie noticed one of the chandeliers lurching sideways, each globe spluttering with the motion. Would the whole contraption fall? The horror of the thought that perhaps it was about to made her mouth dry. Had anyone else seen? To shout out would draw the attention to herself she so wanted to avoid, but the death of some unknowing soul would be for ever on her conscience if she did not.

'Watch out! The light is falling.' Her raised voice carried easily across the chatter around her, but a group of girls to one side were not quite fast enough. With a crash the ironwork of the leaves and flowers caught the leg of a beautiful young blonde woman.

In the chaos Cassie hurried forward, kneeling almost at the same time as another did, bumping his arm against hers.

Monsieur Nathanael Colbert.

Close.

A touch away, unbridled fury in his eyes. Grey eyes with just a hint of blue. Unbalance hit and she felt a jagged panic, her glance taking in the line of his jaw bissected with the scar she'd wrought upon him. When she had last seen this it had been opened red, blood falling across his shirt in a stream. She wanted to reach out and trace it, as if trying through touch to let him know of her sorrow. He would not welcome it, she knew, but betrayal always held two sides and this was one of them.

The sheer physical presence of him scorched at sense but as the woman's cries mounted the healer in Cassie prevailed. She could not deal with the ramifications of meeting Colbert now. Looking down, she placed her palm hard against the back of a shapely knee and the flow of blood waned, red dribbling on to her skirt, the colours mixing strangely.

'Keep still. There is a lot of bleeding and it needs to be stemmed.'

At that the young girl sobbed louder, grasping her free hand in a vice-like grip.

'Will I die?'

'No. A person is able to lose at least twenty per cent of their blood and still feel only mildly cold.'

Leached grey eyes raked across her own, no warmth whatsoever within them.

'How much would you say I have already lost?' The wounded girl's voice was breathless with panic.

Cassandra made a thorough check of the area, lifting her ankle to ascertain just what lay beneath.

'A little over half that amount so it would be wise to stay calm.'

The answering terrified shriek left her ears aching.

'I am certain that it is not so severe, Miss Forsythe.' The voice she had recalled in her dreams for so many years was measured. It was the first time she had ever heard him speak in English, the clipped and rounded vowels of privilege hanging upon every word. She hated the way her heart began to race.

'Well, as your shin has been badly cut it is most important that you...'

A shadow to one side caught her glance and then all she knew was black.

Sandrine Mercier? Speaking perfect English? Downed by the last falling remains of the chandelier and completely unconscious. The loathing he felt for her swelled in his throat. Another deceit. A further lie.

She lay on her side, her eyelashes magnified against the shining de Clare tiles, her hair shorter now, and sleeker. She was still thin, but the beauty once only promised had blossomed into a full and utter radiance.

Damn her.

He wanted to stand and turn away, but to do so would invite question and in his line of work such scrutiny was never a good thing.

Lydia Forsythe was screaming at the very top of her voice, but the bleeding from her leg had almost subsided. A doctor had scurried over as well as her distraught mother and a myriad of friends. Around Sandrine just himself and one girl lingered, an uncertain frown on her forehead and tears pooling in dark-brown eyes.

Albi de Clare, the host of the evening's entertainment, crouched down beside him. 'My God, I cannot understand how this has happened for the lights were installed only a few months ago and I was assured that they were well secured. If you can lift her, Nathaniel, there is a room leading off this one that should offer more privacy.'

Another touch. A further punishment. When Nat brought her into his arms blue-green eyes snapped open to his, horror blossoming into shock.

'I never...faint.'

'You didn't this time, either. The debris from the chandelier hit you.'

She was vibrating with panic, her head turned away. On reaching the smaller salon he placed her down upon a sofa, wishing he could leave.

'My personal physician is amongst the guests, Nathaniel, and he is examining Miss Forsythe as we speak.' Albi de Clare's tone was muted and Nat saw Sandrine's glance flicker round taking in the presence of the others who had followed them in. 'He will come to you next.'

'No.' Already she had swung her feet onto the floor and was sitting there, head in her hands. 'Please do not take the trouble to call him, my lord. I should not wish for any fuss and I already feel so very much...better.' She stood on the word and just as quickly sat down, beads of sweat garnering on her top lip.

Albi, however, was not dissuaded from

seeking a medical opinion, hailing his doctor as he came into the room.

'Mr Collins, could you have a look at this injury? The back of the patient's head has connected with the remains of the lamp.'

The old physician placed his leather satchel on a table next to the sofa before making much of extracting a pair of glasses from an outer pocket and perching them across his nose.

'Certainly, sir. Those outside intimated that you were one of the first on the scene, Lord Lindsay. Was the young lady unconscious for long after this happened?'

'Only for a few seconds,' Nat answered. 'As soon as I picked her up she seemed to regain her mind.' Plain and simple. Everything complex and twisted would come later.

Sitting, the physician held up two fingers.

'How many do you see, my dear?'

'Four.'

The woman beside Sandrine shook her head and worried eyes went quickly to her.

'Three. Two.' Guessing for all her heart's worth.

'Do you have a headache?'

'Just a small one.'

'Is your right arm numb?'

She did not answer as she dug her nails into the flesh above her elbow. So numb she did not feel it at all?

At the doorway a group of interested on-lookers had gathered, though Sandrine, marked by the blood of the other victim, looked bewildered and vulnerable. She had also begun to shake. Badly. Taking off his jacket, Nathaniel tucked it about her, for shock could be as much of an enemy as injury. He hated himself for bothering.

'Warmth will help.'

For the first time he noticed the pendant at her throat, the one he had given her in Saint Estelle before she had betrayed him. The grey fabric of her bodice had drooped to reveal the roundness of one breast and the tall woman who had followed them in knelt down to pull the gown back into place, the skin on her cheeks flaming.

'Keep still, Cassie.'

Cassie? The anger in Sandrine's eyes was magnified by a deep and startling verdant green.

Albi's voice broke into his thoughts. 'If you bring Miss Cassandra this way, Nathaniel, a carriage is waiting. Miss Northrup, if you would collect her reticule and follow us?'

Northrup? Maureen and Cassandra Northrup? These were two of Lord Cowper's daughters? Hell.

A shutter had fallen across her averted eyes at the mention of her name, wariness and the cold surge of alarm evident.

'I need no extra assistance, my lords. My s…sister can help me to our conveyance.'

At that the other moved forward, pleased to be able to do something in the room with all its onlookers and the stark awkward silence.

Within a moment they were gone, both of them, only the scent of some flower he could not name left behind.

Hemlock? Foxgloves? Lily of the Valley? All poisonous and lethal.

Albi watched them go, a frown across his brow. 'The Northrup sisters may have their detractors, but it is my reasoning that with just a little time and effort they could knock the Originals from their perches. They seldom come out into society, but by all accounts their mother was beautiful, too. I think there's a third sister, married and living in Scotland. You will need to get your jacket back.'

'Perhaps.' Nat's tone was flat.

'They live in Upper Brook Street and you can't miss Avalon, the Northrup monstrosity.' Nathaniel did not wait to hear more, walking out instead to the ballroom and being instantly surrounded by the newest and most beautiful débutantes of the season.

Young women of impeccable taste and good breeding, their pasts unblemished and flawless. He smiled as he moved into their midst.

Cassie's head ached and her neck stung. She knew the wax from the candle globes had burnt her, but there had been too much to ascertain about the health of the young woman to spend time thinking about her own injuries.

Lord Lindsay.

The physician had called him that and de Clare had named him Nathaniel. Lord Nathaniel Lindsay, the heir apparent to the earldom of St Auburn. She could not believe it, could not quite take in that her dangerous rescuer in Nay with his scarred body and quick reflexes was now a dandified lord, known across all of England for his wealth and his power, with family lineage stretching back across the centuries.

Away from the stares, Cassie was feeling a

lot better. The borrowed coat was warm, her shivers lessened by the touch of wool. She could smell him, too, here in the carriage, the depth of him and the strength and if her sister had not been right there beside her she might have breathed in further, allowing the colours of his beauty to explode inside, tantalising and teasing.

The scent of a man who could ruin her.

As the skin at her neck smarted beneath the heavy silk swathe of her gown, Cassie longed to take off her clothes and walk into the shallow pool at Avalon. Her mother's pool, Alysa's gown still upon the hook and her beads draped across a single gold-leafed chair. Papa had insisted on them staying.

'Lord Lindsay has only recently returned to the social scene, but I have heard tales about him.' Maureen watched her sister carefully, and Cassie knew that she was curious.

'Tales?'

'He is said to have spent some time in France. You did not meet him there, did you? I gained the impression he knew you.'

Cassandra shook her head, the truth too terrible to speak of, and she pulled the jacket in tighter.

He had remembered her, she knew he had, and under the smile she wore to keep Maureen's avid curiosity at bay she also knew she must stay as far from him as possible.

When the lights of Avalon came into view she was pleased to see them.

Nathaniel Lindsay watched the house through the night, the moon upon its burnished roof outlining the gables and the attics.

The Gothic style here in London. Even the trees had taken their cue from the stark outline of the building and dropped some of their leaves as though it were already winter.

He should not be here, of course, but memory had made him come, the calm treachery of Sandrine's voice in Perpignan as she had dispatched him into hell.

'I barely know him, but he is a soldier of France, so better to leave him alive. But do as you will, I really don't care.'

Swearing, he turned away, but not before the pale outline of a figure holding a candle moved through the second floor, down the stairs and out on to the porch, peering through the black of night.

There was no way she could have seen him,

tucked into the shadow of a brick wall. But for a second before she blew out the flame the world seemed bathed in a daylight born from the candle, and she looked right into the heart of him.

Then there was only darkness and she was gone.

Sometimes his world disgorged ghosts from the past, but never ones as worrying as Sandrine Mercier. He'd been twenty when he had entered the heady enclave of espionage, his grandfather's distant demeanour a catalyst for him to become part of a close group of men who worked for the British Service.

His friend, Stephen Hawkhurst, had already been involved and when Nathaniel's grandfather, the Earl of St Auburn, had ranted and raved about his uselessness as the only son and heir, Nathaniel had joined as well.

Determining the likelihood of the rumoured marriages between the Spanish and French crowns had bought Nat into France, his expertise in both languages allowing him an easy access to the higher and lower echelons of its society.

The ties that were being forged between Britain and France were becoming strained, leaving a climate of suspicion and fear in their wake. A united block would render England isolated and make the battle for the control of Europe all that much harder to fight.

Nathaniel's mission had been to test the waters, so to speak, and to liaise with the handful of British agents who had been assimilated into the French way of life, keeping an eye on the workings of a political ally who was hard to trust.

Determining the likelihood of such an alliance had taken him to the court of Madrid. Returning across the Pyrenees to make his way up into Paris, he had been alarmed at the murder of one of his agents whilst on the road to Bayonne. Finding those culpable had led him into an enclave of French bandits near Lourdes.

And it was here he had met Sandrine.

Cassandra knew he was there, quiet and hidden in the night. It had been the same at Nay, when in the chaos the spaces around him had been full of a certain resolve, menacing and dangerous, the last afternoon light glinting in the dark of his hair as he had taken apart the minions of Anton Baudoin.

She shivered at the name and thought of

Celeste. A week sooner and her cousin might have lived as well, might have been taken too, through the long night and back into warmth. She did not know Lord Lindsay was an Englishman then, dressed in the trousers of a peasant, skin sliced with the marks of war. The French bastards had not known it either, his accent from the warmer climate of the south and the musical lilt of a Provençal childhood masking all that he was.

Nathanael. He had named himself such. Monsieur Nathanael Colbert. At least part of his name had been true. His hands had been harder then, marked with the calluses of a labouring man and none of the softer lord on show. He still wore the same ring though, a gold chevron against blue, on the fourth finger of his right hand.

A movement behind made her turn.

'Ma'am, Katie is crying and Elizabeth cannot make her stop.'

One of the Northrup maids stood in the doorway, a heavy frown evident, and, forcing all the thoughts from her mind, Cassie hurried inside.

Tonight, chaos felt close and Lord Lindsay was a large part of the reason. She understood that with a heartfelt clarity as the cries of the girl took Cassie from her revelries.

Elizabeth, her maid, was in the annex at the rear of the house, the place used when women needed a bed for a night or two before being rehomed elsewhere. She was bathing the burns on thin legs, angry red scarring beneath the soft brush of cotton; another small casualty owing her injuries to London's underbelly of child trading.

'Did you make certain your hands were clean, Lizzie, before you touched the wounds?'

'I did, ma'am.'

'And you used the lime solution?'

'Just as you told me, ma'am.'

The smell of it was still in the air, sharp and strong, crawling into all the corners of the room. Alysa, Cassie's French mother, had always been a vehement supporter of cleanliness when dealing with sickness, and such teachings were ingrained within Cassie.

Soaping up her hands, she dried them and felt the child's forehead. Fever was settling in, the flush in Katie's cheeks ruddy and marked. Removing a clean apron from a hook by the door, Cassie put it on and went to stand beside Katie, the folds of the child's skin weeping and swollen. Carefully Cassie took plump shards of green from her medical cabinet and squeezed the slime into a pestle and mortar before spitting into the mixture. Mama had shown her this and the procedure took her mind back unwillingly into a different time and place.

She had been almost eighteen years old, still a girl, still hopeful, still imbued with the possibilities of life.

Completely foolish.

Utterly naive.

And painfully heartsick from the guilt of her mother's death.

Chapter Two

Nay, Languedoc-Roussillon, France—October 1846

The stranger had forced himself into stillness. She could see it as he stood, his heart and breath calmed by pure will-power as he raised his blade and stepped forward.

So many were dead or dying; such a little space of time between the living and the departed and Cassandra expected that she would be next.

A knife she had retrieved from the ground felt solid in her fist and the wind was behind her. Left handed. Always an advantage. But the rain made steel slippery as he parried and the mud under her feet finished the job. As she fell her hat spun off into the grey and her plait unfolded into silence. She saw the disbelief in his eyes, the hesitation and the puzzlement, his knife angling to miss her slender neck, pale against all else that was not.

The shot behind sounded loud, too loud, and she could smell the flare of powder for just a second before he fell, flesh punched with lead.

He could have killed her easily, she thought, as she scrambled up and snatched back her cap, angry with herself for taking another look at his face.

Mud could not mask the beauty of him, nor could the pallor of death. She wished he might have been old and ugly, a man to forget after a second of seeing, but his lips were full and his lashes were long and in his cheek she could see the dent of a dimple.

A man who would not bring his blade in battle through the neck of a woman? Even a fallen one such as she? The shame in her budded against the futility of his gesture and she went to turn away. Once she might have cared more, might have wept for such a loss of life and beauty and goodness. But not now.

The movement of his hand astonished her.

'He is alive.' Even as she spoke she wished she had not.

'Kill the bastard, then. Finish him off.'

Her fingers felt for a pulse, strong against the beat of time, blood still coursing through a body marked with wounds. Raising the knife, she caught the interest of Baudoin behind and, moving to block his view, brought the blade down hard. The earth jarred her wrist through the thin woollen edge of his jacket and she almost cried out, but didn't.

'Take your chances.' Whispered beneath her breath, beneath the wind and the rain and the grey empty nothingness. Tonight it would snow. He would not stand a hope. Cleaning the knife against her breeches, she stood.

'You did well, *ma chère*.' Baudoin moved forward to cradle the curve of her chest, and the same anger that had been her companion for all of the last months tasted bitter in her mouth.

She knew what would come next by the flare in his eyes, knew it the moment he hit her, his sex hardened by death, blood and fear, but he had forgotten the knife in her palm and in his haste had left her fighting arm free.

A mistake. She used the brutality of his ardour as he took her to the ground, the blade slipping through the space between his ribs to enter his heart and when she rolled him off her into the mud and stood, she stomped down hard upon his fingers.

'For Celeste.' She barely recognised her voice and made an effort to tether in her panic. The snow would help her, she was sure of it; tracks could be hidden beneath the white and the winter was only just beginning.

'And…for you, too.' The sound was quiet at first, almost gone in the high keening of wind, a whisper through great pain and much effort.

Her assailant, his grey eyes bloodshot and sweat on his brow underpinning more extensive injuries. When he heaved himself up, she saw he was a big man, the muscle in his arms pressed tight against the fabric of his jacket.

'You killed him too cleanly, *mademoiselle.*' Not a compliment either as he glanced at Anton Baudoin. 'I would have made him suffer.'

He knew how much she had hated him, the prick of pity behind his eyes inflating her fury. No man would ever hold such power over her again.

'Here.' He held out a silver flask, the stopper emblazoned with a crest. 'Drink this. It will help.'

She meant to push it back at him, refusal a

new capacity, but sense kept her quiet. Half a dozen days by foot to safety through mountainous land she held no measure of. Fools would perish and she was not a fool.

The spirits were warm, slung as the metal had been against his skin. The crest surprised her. Had he stolen it in some other skirmish? She could feel the unfamiliar fire of the whisky burn right down into her stomach.

'Who was he?'

'A bandit. His name was Anton Baudoin.'

'And these others?'

'His men.'

'You were alone with them?' Now his eyes only held the savage gleam of anger. For him or for her, she could not tell. Against the backdrop of a storm he looked far more dangerous than any man she had ever seen.

As if he could read her mind, he spoke. 'Stop shaking. I don't rape young girls.'

'But you often kill men?'

At that, he smiled. 'Killing is easy. It's the living that's difficult.'

Shock overtook her, all the horror of the past minutes and months robbing her of breath and sense. She was a murderer. She was a murderer with no place to run to and no hope at safety.

He was wrong. Everything was difficult. Life was humiliating, exhausting and shameful. And now she was bound for hell.

The tall stranger took a deep swallow from the flask before replacing the lid. Then he laid his jacket on the ground, raising his shirt to see the damage. Blood dripped through a tear in the flesh above his hipbone. Baudoin's shot, she thought. It had only just missed killing him. With much care he stooped and cut a wide swathe of fabric from the shirttails of one of the dead men, slicing it into long ribbons of white.

Bandages. He had tied them together with intricate knots in seconds and without pausing began to wind the length tightly around his middle. She knew it must have hurt him to do so, but not in an expression, word or gesture did he allow her the knowledge of that, simply collecting his clothes on finishing and shrugging back into them.

Then he disappeared into the house behind, and she could hear things being pulled this way and that, the sound of crashing furniture and upturned drawers. He was looking for something, she was sure of it, though for the life of her she could not imagine what it might be. Money? Weapons?

A few moments later and he was back again, empty-handed.

'I am heading for Perpignan if you want to come.' Tucking a gun and powders into his belt, he repositioned his knife into a sheath of leather. Already the night was coming down upon them and the trees around the clearing seemed darker and more forbidding. The cart he had used to inveigle his way into the compound stood a little way off, the wares he plied meagre: pots, pans and rolls of fabric amidst sacks of flour and sugar.

She had no idea as to who he was or what he was or why he was in Nay. He could be worse than any man here ever had been or he could be like her uncle and father, honourable and decent.

A leaf fell before her, twirling in the breeze. *If it rests on its top, I will not go with him*, she thought, even as the veins of the underside stilled in the mud. *And if he insists that I accompany him, I will strike out the other way.*

But he only turned into the line of bushes behind and melted into green, his cart gouging trails in the mud.

A solid indication of direction, she thought, like a sign or a portent or an omen of safety. Gathering up her small bundle of things, she followed him into the gloom.

There was no simple way to tie a neckcloth, Nathaniel thought, no easy shortcut that might allow him the time for another drink before he went out. Already the clock showed ten, and Hawk would be waiting. Catching sight of his reflection in the mirror, he frowned.

His valet had outdone himself with tonight's dress, the dizzying hues of his waistcoat clashing with the coloured silk of his cravat; a fashionable man with nothing else to occupy his mind save entertainment. People dropped their guards around men such as this. His fingers tightened against the ebony of his cane and he felt for the catch hidden beneath the rim at the back as he walked downstairs.

He had returned from France in the early months of 1847 more damaged than he allowed others to know and had subsequently been attached to the London office. For a while the change had been just what he needed, the small problems of wayward politicians or corrupt businessmen an easy task to deal with after the mayhem of Europe.

Such work barely touched him. It was simple to shadow the unscrupulous and bring them to the notice of the law, the degenerate fraudsters and those who operated outside justice effortlessly discovered.

Aye, he thought. He could have done the work with his hands tied and a blindfold on until a month ago when two women had been dragged from the Thames with their throats cut. Young women and both dressed well.

No one had known them. No one had missed them. No anxious family member had contacted the police. It was as though they had come into the river without a past and through the teeming throng of humanity around the docklands without a footprint.

The only clue Nat had been able to garner was from an urchin who had sworn he had seen a toff wiping blood from a blade beside the St Katharine Docks. A tall and well-dressed man, the boy had said, before scurrying off into the narrow backstreets.

Stephen Hawkhurst had been asked to look into the case as well, and the Venus Club rooms five roads away towards the city had caught their attention.

'The members meet here every few weeks. They are gentlemen mostly with a great appetite for the opposite sex. By all accounts they pay for dancers and singers and other women who think nothing of shedding their clothes for entertainment.'

'So it could be one of them is using the club for more dubious pursuits,' Nat expanded. 'There are a number of men whose names and faces I recognise.'

He had kept a close eye on the comings and goings from the club across the past weeks, astonished at the numerous alliances taking place. 'Any accusations would need to be carefully handled, though, for some there have genuine political and social standing.'

'Hard to get closer without causing comment, you mean?' Stephen questioned.

'Exactly. But if we joined we could blend in.'

Stephen had not believed him serious. 'I don't think belonging to the ranks of the Venus Club is the sort of distinction one would want to be known for.'

'It's a place hiding secrets, Hawk, and privacy is highly valued.'

'Well, I'm not taking part in any initiation or rites of passage.'

Each of them had laughed.

'Frank Booth is reported to be a member. I will ask him to sponsor us.'

A week later they were given a date, a time and a place, a small break in a case that was baffling. Girls were ruined all the time in London, for reasons of economics, for the want of food, for a roof over the head of a child born out of wedlock. But they were seldom so brutally hurt.

Sandrine. He remembered her ruined hand and the fear in her face when he had first met her.

The rage inside him began to build. Back then Cassandra Northrup had never given him any glimpse of an identity, though with each and every day in her company questions had woven their way into the little that she told him.

The first night had been the worst. She had cried behind him in small sobs, unstoppable over miles of walking in the dark. He had not helped her because he couldn't. The wound in his side had ached like the devil, fiery-hot and prickling, and by midnight he knew that he would have to rest.

Throwing down the few things he had taken from the cart after abandoning it many miles back, he leaned against a tree, the bark of its trunk firm behind him. Already the whirling circles of giddiness threatened, the ache at his hip sending pins and needles into his chest.

The girl sat on the other side of the small clearing, tucked into a stiff and inconsolable shape.

'You are safer than you were before. I said I would not hurt you.' He couldn't understand her weeping.

'I killed a man.'

'He was about to rape you.' Nat's heart sank at the implications of her guilt. God, how long had it been since he had felt anything remotely similar? He wished he had been the one to slide a knife into the French miscreant, for he would have gutted him and enjoyed watching him die. Slowly.

Her hands crossed her heart and her lips moved as if reciting a prayer.

Had the bullet wound not hurt as much he might have laughed, might have crossed the space between them and shaken her into sense. But he could only sit and watch and try to mitigate his pain.

'I am sure that the wrath of God takes intent into account.'

'Oh, I intended to kill him.' Honestly said. Given back in a second and no hesitation in it.

'I was thinking more of your assailant's purpose. I do not think Monsieur Baudoin would have been gentle with you.'

'Yet two wrongs do not make a right?'

He closed his eyes and felt the bloom of fatigue, irritation rising at her unreasonableness. 'If you had not killed him, I would have. One way or another he would have been dead. If it helps, pretend I did it.'

'Who are you?' The green in her eyes under moonlight matched the dark of the trees. In the daylight they were bluer, changeable.

'Nathanael Colbert. A friend.' Barked out, none of the empathy he knew she wanted held within the word. She remained silent, a small broken shape in the gloom, tucked up against bracken, the holes in the leather soles of her shoes easily seen from this angle. 'Why the hell were you there in the first place?'

He did not think she would answer as the

wind came through into the hollow, its keening sound as plaintive as her voice.

'They caught us a long time ago.' He saw her counting on her fingertips as she said it, the frown upon her brow deepening. Months? Years?

'Us?'

He had seen no other sign of captives.

'Celeste and I.'

Hell. Another girl. 'Where is she?'

'Dead.' The flat anger in her voice was cold.

'Recently?'

She nodded, her expression gleamed in sadness. She had old bruises across her cheek and new ones on her hand. In the parting of her hair when her cap had been dislodged he had seen the opaque scar of a wound that could have so easily killed her.

As damaged as he was.

Tonight he did not have the energy to know more of her story and the thin wanness was dispiriting. If they could have a drink things would be better, but the flask he had brought with him was long since empty.

'Can you hear that stream?'

She nodded.

'We need water…?'

He left the words as a question. No amount of want in the world could get him standing. He had lost too much blood and he knew it.

'Do you have the flask?'

'Here.'

When she took it and left he closed his eyes and tried to find some balance in the silence. He wanted to tend to himself, but he would need water to do that. And fire. He wondered if the young French captive would be able to follow his instructions when she returned.

He also wondered just exactly how those at Nay had gained their information on the identity and movements of a British agent who had long been a part of the fabric of French country life.

It was quiet in the trees and all the grief of losing Celeste flooded back. Her cousin's body rounded with child. Her eyes lifeless. The pain of it surged into Cassie's throat, blocking breath, and she stopped to lean against a tree. The anguish of life and death. What was it the man who sat in the clearing wrapped in bandages had said?

Killing is easy. It's the living that is difficult.

Perhaps, after all, he was right. Perhaps

Celeste had known that, too, and put an end to all that she had loathed, taking the child to a place that was better but leaving her here alone.

Alone in a world where everything looked bleak. Bleaker than bleak even under the light of a small moon, the trickle of water at her feet running into the tattered remains of her boots and wetting her toes. The cold revived a little of her fight, reminded her how in the whole of those eight terrible months she had not given up, had not surrendered. She wished the stream might have been deeper so that she could have simply stripped off and washed away sin. A baptism. A renewal. A place to begin yet again and survive.

The flask in hand reminded her of purpose and she knelt to the water.

Her companion looked sick, the crusted blood beneath his nails reflected in the red upon his clothes, sodden through the layers of bandage. Without proper medicine how could he live? Water would clean the wound, but what could be done for any badness that might follow? The shape of leaves in the moonlight on the other side of the river suddenly caught her attention. Maudeline. Her mother had used this very plant in her concoctions. An astringent, she had said. A cleanser. A natural gift from the hands of a God who placed his medicines where they were most needed.

The small bank was easy to climb and, taking a handful of the plant, she stripped away the woody stems, the minty scent adding certainty to her discovery. She remembered this fresh sweet smell from Alysa's rooms and was heartened by the fact. The work of finding enough leaves and tucking them into her pocket took all her concentration, purpose giving energy. A small absolution. A task she had done many hundreds of times under the guidance of her mother.

An anchor to the familiar amidst all that was foreign. She needed this stranger in a land she held no measure of and he needed her. An equal support. It had been so long since she had felt any such worthiness.

He was asleep when she returned, though the quiet fall of her feet woke him.

'I have maudeline for your injury.' Bringing out the leaves, she began to crush them between her fingers, mixing them to a paste with the water on a smooth rock she had wiped down before using. She saw how he watched her, his grey eyes never leaving the movement of her hands.

'Are you a witch, then?'

She laughed, the sound hoarse and rough after so many months of disuse. 'No, but Mama was often thought to be.'

Again she saw the dimple in his right cheek, the deep pucker of mirth making her smile.

'Maudeline? I have not heard of it.'

'Another name for it is camphor.'

He nodded and came up on to his knees, holding his head in his hands as though a headache had suddenly blossomed.

'It hurts you?'

'No.' Squeezed out through pain.

When he stood she thought he looked unsteady, but she simply watched as he gathered sticks and set to making a fire. The tinder easily caught, the snake of smoke and then flame. Using the bigger pieces of branch he built it up until even from a distance she could feel the radiating warmth.

'The tree canopy will dissipate the smoke,' he said after a few moments. 'The low cloud will take care of the rest.'

Half an hour later flame shadow caught at his torso as he removed his shirt, the bandages following. His wound showed shattered skin, the tell-tale red lines of inflammation already radiating.

'Don't touch.' Her directive came as she saw he was about to sear the edges of skin together with a glowing stick. 'It is my belief that dirt kills a man with more certainty than a bullet and I can tell it is infected.'

Crossing to him, she wiped her hands with the spare leaves and poured water across the sap. When she touched him she knew he had the fever. Another complication. A further problem.

'I have been ill like this before and lived.' He had seen her frown.

Lots of 'befores', she mused, lines of crossed white opaque scars all over his body. The thought made her careful.

'You are a soldier?'

He only laughed.

Or a criminal, she thought, for what manner of man looked as he did? When he handed over the flask of water, she did not take a drink.

'I will heat it to clean the wound. It might hurt for it has been left a while. If you had some leather to bite down upon…?''

He broke into her offered advice. 'I will cope.'

* * *

Stephen Hawkhurst's voice made Nathaniel start, the echo around the marbled lobby disconcerting as all the years past rolled back into the present.

'You look as though you have the problems of the world upon your shoulders, Nat. Still thinking of the Northrup chit, I'd be guessing: fine eyes, a fine figure and a sense of mystery. Her uncle, Reginald Northrup, will be at the Venus Club tonight. Perhaps you can find out more about her from him.'

'Perhaps.'

'A few years ago when I was in Paris I heard a rumour about a woman who sounded remarkably like Cassandra Northrup.'

'What did it say?'

'That she was kept a prisoner in southern France and that she was not released for quite some time.'

'I see.'

'Her rescuer was also mentioned in detail.' The flint of gold in his friend's eyes was telling and there was a certain question there.

'It was you, Nat, wasn't it? And she was one of theirs?

'Whose?'

'The French. One of their agents.'

Anger sliced in a quick rod of pain. 'No, Cassandra Northrup never held loyalty to any cause save that of her own.'

'Others here might disagree with you. She is the chairwoman of the charity Daughters of the Poor.'

'Prostitutes?'

Hawk nodded, leaving Nat to ponder on how the circles of life turned around in strange patterns.

'She must have been a child then, and scared. God, even now she looks young. And you got home in one piece, after all.'

One piece? How little Stephen truly knew.

Taking his hat and cloak from the doorman, Nat forced away his recollections and walked out into a cold and windy London night.

They were all there, myriad affluent men gathered in a room that looked much like a law chamber or a place of business. Nat was glad that Stephen stood beside him because he still felt dislocated and detached, thrown by the reappearance of a woman he had thought never to see again.

He recalled Cassandra Northrup's eyes were exactly the same as they had been, guarded in their turquoise, shuttered by care and secrets. But her hair had changed from the wild curls she had once favoured and she was far more curvaceous.

If her eyes had not given her away her left hand would have, of course, with the half-finger and the deep scar across the rest of her knuckles.

It had been a newer wound back then in the clearing, when she had reached forward and laid one cool palm across his back. He had flinched as she brought the knife she carried upwards to cut away the badness.

The pain had made him sweat, hot incandescence in the cool of night as she simply tipped the heated flask up and covered ragged open flesh.

The camphor helped, as did her hands threading through places on his spine that seemed to transfer the pain. Surprise warred with agony under her adept caresses.

The poultice was sticky and the new bandages she bound the ointment with were from the bottom of her shirt. Cleaner. Softer. He could smell her on them.

He wished that he had the whisky to dull the pain. He wished for a bed that was not on a forest floor, but some place warmer, more comfortable, some place where his heartbeat did not rattle against the cold hard of earth.

'If you sit, it should help with the drainage.'

He was shivering now, substantially, and went to drape his jacket around himself to find warmth, but she held it away and shook her head.

'You are burning up. The mind plays tricks when the fever rages and as I cannot shift you to the stream we will have to make do with the cold night air instead. I had hoped it would snow.'

Her accent was Parisian, the inflection of the drawing rooms and the society salons where anything and everything was possible. He wondered why the hell she should have been in Nay, dressed in the clothes of a lad, and when he inadvertently blurted the thought out aloud, he saw her flinch.

'I think you should sleep, Monsieur Colbert.'

His name. Not quite right. But he needed to be quiet and he needed to think. There was danger here. He wished he could have asked her who she was, what she was, but the camphor was winding its way into the quick pricks of pain and he closed his eyes to block her from him.

He would be sore in the morning if he lived. The wound or the fever could kill him, but it was the bleeding that she was most concerned about. She had not been able to stop it. Already blood pooled beneath him, more hindrance to a body struggling with survival.

Tipping up the flask, she took the last drops of water.

She was starving. She was exhausted. The embers of the fire still glowed in the dark, but outside the small light the unknown gathered.

Baudoin had not existed alone and she knew that others would follow. Oh, granted, this stranger had hidden their tracks well ever since leaving Nay, his cart discarded quite early in the piece. She had watched him set false lures into other directions, the heavy print of a foot in a stream, a broken twig snagged with the hair from her plait, but she knew it would only be a matter of time before those in France's underworld would find them.

She held far too many secrets, that was the problem. She had seen some of the documents

Baudoin's brother had inadvertently left in Celeste's chamber, documents she knew had been taken from the carriage of a murdered man on the road towards Bayonne. A mistake of lust and an error that would lead to all that had happened next.

Her fault. Everything was her fault and her cousin had not even known it. The same familiar panic engulfed her, made her lean forward to catch breath, trying in the terror to hold on to the reason of why Celeste had done as she did. Cassie still felt the sticky blood across her fingers, the warmth of life giving way to cold.

Softly she began to sing, keeping herself staunch; the 'Marseillaise' because it was fast paced and because it was in French.

To arms, citizens,
Form your battalions,
We march, we march...

Celeste was dead. And the Baudoin brothers. How quickly circumstances changed. In a heartbeat. In a breath. She looked across to the stranger, Colbert, and determined that he was still in the land of the living before she shut her eyes.

* * *

The girl was asleep, her hat pulled down across her head and her jacket stretched over the bend of her knees. As Nathaniel looked at her in repose there was a vulnerability apparent that was not evident when she was awake. She was thin, painfully so, and dirty. On a closer inspection he saw on her clothes the handiwork of small, finely taken stitches covering rips and larger holes. Her shirt was buttoned to the throat and the jacket she wore was tightly closed. More than a few sizes too large, it held the look of a military coat without any of the braiding. He knew she still had the knife, but it was not visible anywhere. Too big for the pockets, he imagined it tucked in under her forearm or secreted in one of the boots she wore beneath loose trousers.

A child-woman lost into the vagaries of a war that could not have been kind.

He felt stronger, a surprising discovery this, given his fever, and although the wound tugged when he shifted it did not sting like it had. Still, his vision blurred as he stood from the loss of blood or his own body's heat, he knew not which.

Camphor. Perhaps there was something in the doctoring, some healing property that would confound even the best of physicians? He resolved to use it again.

She stirred across from him, wild curls escaping from the plait and falling around her face. In sleep she looked softer, the burden of life not marking the spaces between her eyes. Her ruined left hand sat on top of the right one and fire outlined the hurt in flame. Not a little injury and not an accident either. This looked to be deliberate, a brutal act of damage that would have taken weeks to heal. It was strange to see such a battle scar on one so young. His own back was filled with the vestige of war, but he had been in the arena of secrets for some time and such damage was to be expected.

Her eyes flicked open suddenly, taking him in, fear reverting to wariness.

'How do you feel?' Even fresh from sleep she was observant.

'Better.'

Her glance at his throat read the measured beat of his heart. 'Your temperature is still high so you should be drinking as much as you can. In a moment I will fetch more water.'

A frown of concern slashed the girl's fore-head, but he was tired of thinking of her as 'the girl'. 'What are you called?'

'Sandrine Mercier.'

Rolling the name on his tongue, he liked the sound of it. 'How old are you?'

'Almost eighteen.' Surprisingly forthcoming, though she did not look to have as many years as she professed.

'And your cousin?'

Moonlight caught her face as her chin lifted. 'Celeste was twenty and she loved music. She loved everything beautiful and charming and good. She played the piano and sang like an angel…' Her voice came to a halt.

Nat knew what she was doing because he had done the same himself when those close to him had died. A memory they might be, but in speech they came alive, drawn for others to know, almost living.

'Did Baudoin kill her?'

Only the quick shake of her head.

One day she will be beautiful, he thought. One day she will take men's hearts and break them. For now she was young. Too young for him. For now the stamp of grace lay in her long limbs and her boyish defiance, the promise of womanhood only hinted at.

He turned away, not wishing for her to see his regard.

He was back to being angry, his eyes the colour of a storm, not dark, not light, but the in-between shade that spoke of rain and coldness.

'Are you a part of Guy Lebansart's circle of spies?' If she found out something about him, there might be protection there.

His interest ignited. 'Spies?'

'Men who would take secrets and use them.'

'For France?'

'Or for whoever is paying the most.'

His frown deepened. 'Did you ever know any of these secrets, Sandrine?' In his words she could hear exactly what she did not want to. Interest and intrigue. Eight months in captivity had taught her every nuance in the language of deception.

'No.' She kept her voice bland and low, shaking out the truth with effort. 'I was only a prisoner.'

'Where did they keep you?'

She did not answer, moving instead to retrieve the flask. Her mattress had been in a room off Celeste and Louis's chamber, a sanctuary she tried very hard to seldom leave. Lying low, she only ever ventured out when the early hours of the morning saw each inhabitant befuddled by strong drink, her cousin included. But Celeste had made her own bargain with the devil and had won conditions to make the tenure livable. Cassie's thoughts went again to Celeste's beautiful voice and her smile. When memory was selective, everything was easier.

'I will get water and then we should leave. If others follow—'

He cut off her worry with two words.

'They won't.'

The confidence of a victor. So fragile. So absolutely flimsy. Baudoin had said no one would ever dare to challenge him and look at what had happened. Her French uncle had been certain, too, of the route west and then lost his way into peril.

Everyone could be bought for the price of pain or promise or vanity. She wondered what Monsieur Nathanael Colbert's price might be. Her own was freedom and she would never give it up again for anyone.

'When we reach the next town, hide your face with this.' He tossed her a scarf, dirtied with dust and blood. 'And tuck your hair well into the crown of your hat. If anyone asks a question of you, look stupid, for there is safeguard in a simple mind. If you could walk with more of a swagger—'

She cut him off. 'I know what to do.'

He swore at that, roundly, and began to collect his things.

Reginald Northrup was a large man, his face florid and his smile showing a mouth with at least a few teeth missing. The brandy he had hold of was in a glass as oversized as he was. The sweat on his brow reflected the light above him.

'It is a surprise to see you here, Lindsay. I hear you aided my niece the other evening at the de Clare ball?'

The man who sat near Northrup turned to hear his answer.

'Indeed. The last pieces of a falling chandelier knocked her unconscious and a doctor was called.'

'I am certain Cassandra herself could have remedied any wound she received. She has a knack for the healing and her mother was just the same.'

'Her mother was reputed to be one of society's beauties, was she not?' Hawk's question. Nat could not quite let go of the thought that he had voiced the query for his benefit.

'She was, but Alysa Northrup died a good many years ago when one of her science experiments went wrong. Had she lived a century ago she might have been burned at the stake as a witch, for there were rumblings in all quarters about her unusual endeavours and none of them was kind.'

The easygoing stance of the man hardened, giving Nat an impression of much emotion.

'She was a beautiful woman, Reg.' Lord Christopher Hanley, sitting next to Reginald, had imbibed too much strong drink, lending his speech an air of openness. 'None of the other débutantes that year could touch her in brains or beauty. I thought for a time it was you she was sweet upon until your brother snaffled her up right under your very nose and made her his wife.'

Northrup seemed out of step with such a confidence. 'Both girls are as odd as their mother was. You will do yourself a favour by staying out of the way of them, Lindsay. Indeed, most gentlemen in society have done so already.'

Hawk beside him laughed. 'I think it might be the other way around, sir, for even though they seldom venture into the social realm your nieces rebuff all interested parties with alacrity.'

'If they turn their noses up at everything, it is because their father has too little left of his wits to bid them marry. Maureen has already reached a grand old age and I fear that she will always remain a spinster. Rodney, their brother, shall have to no doubt house them when he inherits the properties.'

By the look on Reginald Northrup's face Nathaniel judged that he was not pleased about the fact. The terms of an entailment, perhaps, that left him with little to fall back upon?

'The younger daughter was married in France, if memory serves me well? I remember it as quite a scandal at the time, Reg, and she never took on his name.' Hanley spoke again, and Nathaniel stiffened. Another ache hooking into the cold prick of betrayal. He wondered what she had done with the ring he had given her, his mother's ring, a single, pure, verdant emerald set in white gold.

'What was the story of her groom?' Nat addressed Reginald Northrup directly.

'Oh, up and gone by all accounts, for she arrived home in a melancholic state that took a good year to recover from. I doubt any new husband would have put up with such gloom for that length of time, though my brother was happy enough to have her back and never questioned the marriage. He lives in his own world of science and experiments much the same as his wife was wont to. It was this interest that drew them together in the first place, I suppose.'

The layers of truth peeled back and, within the Venus Club in a room gilded with ostentation and excess, Nat found himself disheartened. It was what had happened after that which Nathaniel failed to understand: the closeness and then the unfathomable distance. He shook away his thoughts as Hawk spoke again.

'Reginald is asking if we wish to join him at his country home for the Venus Club's August celebrations, Nat. I said we would be more than delighted to accept his offer.'

'Indeed.' The taste of bitterness in Nathaniel's mouth was strong, for nothing here made sense to him. Why had Cassandra Northrup never married again given the fragile and unorthodox legality of their nuptials?

She was beautiful. More beautiful than any other woman of the *ton*, even in the dreary guise of a widow. Aye, muted dove-grey suited the tone of her skin and the colour of her eyes and hair.

Her hair had been longer once, falling to the line of her hips in a single swathe of darkened silk as they had pulled themselves out of the river.

He had realised the danger the moment they awoke in the barn they had found in the late afternoon of the day before after walking for many miles. A sense of threat permeated the early morning air, and he was a man who had always relied on instinct.

Sandrine had stirred as he stood, straw from the beds they had fashioned still in the threads of her hair. Everything about her was delicate. Her hands, her nails, the tilt of her chin as she listened.

'Someone is here?'

'More than one. They do not know we are inside, however, or their voices would be quieter.'

He saw how she drew the knife from her sleeve and held it at the ready. Her hands were shaking.

Six of them, he determined, from the footsteps and the whicker of horses. By himself he would have taken them on, but with Sandrine to protect…?

Placing a finger to his lips he drew her to one side of the building and indicated a hole at the bottom of the boards.

'Crawl through and make for the river. If they see you keep running and jump. Stay in the middle where the water flows fastest for at least a mile. After that I will find you.'

Fear sparked in her eyes. 'I cannot swim well.'

'Just put your arms out to each side and relax…'

He did not finish because a shout interrupted them and Nat knew their tracks had been discovered.

'Go.'

A quick nod and the space where she had been was filled only with the scent of her and the sound of someone lifting the catch upon the door.

Unsheathing his knife Nat breathed out, another blade at his belt tilted so that the hilt was easily accessible. The dry straw also caught his eye. He would not make this easy for them and a fire would buy them some time. He hoped to God that Sandrine had reached the water way undetected.

She heard the commotion in the barn as flame leapt from straw, hot through the missing frame of a window.

Colbert had set the place on fire and as a diversion the plan was inspired. Already she saw two of the men retreating, their attention caught so firmly on the blaze they did not notice her as she ran past a line of weeping willows to the river bank.

Where was he? Why had he not come out after her? How long could a person breathe in the smoke and flame of straw? The quick report of a gun sent her under into the cold, down amongst the green of weed and the dirty swirl of mud. She pushed up and away, using her hands as he had told her, spread out as wings, the surface finally in sight, a faint glitter of day where only darkness had been and then she was out, air in her lungs again, a promontory cutting off any sight of the burning barn and distance-dulling noise.

Warm tears of fright ran against the chill, the quick rush of water taking her faster and faster, and the bank a good many yards from her on either side.

Had Nathanael Colbert died in the fight? The wound in his side and the remains of the fever would have sapped his strength and yet he had made sure she had the chance of safety before seeing to his own. He only knew her from her time with Baudoin, a girl marked with the horror of it and yet he had done this for her. Without question.

She wished he was here, behind her, as she was forced along in the rapid current, dragged down with the heaviness of her oversized boots.

And then he was there, reaching for her as she went under yet again, the water in her throat making her cough.

'Put your arms around my neck.'

He was solid and sturdy, the muscles in his shoulders keeping her up in the cold air. His hair had been released from the band he kept it secured with and was falling in wet strands down his back. She wondered how he could keep going as the water flow quickened and rocks appeared, the fall of the river changing and whitening into rapids.

'Don't let go,' he called over his shoulder, one hand fending off a jagged outcrop as they bounced into its path. Then they were free again, down onto a new level of river, softer and quieter.

Cassie could tell he was tiring, the gulps of air he took ragged and uneven. Blood from his wound stained the water crimson about them as damaged flesh opened to pressure. But still he did not stop, waiting until the bushes turned again to countryside before striking in for shore.

The mud under her feet was thick and deep as she gained a purchase. For a good long while they lay there, on the bank, the greyness of the sky above them promising rain. Freezing.

'Take…your clothes…off.' Even he was shivering.

The first soft drift of snow came unexpectedly, landing on her upturned face in a cold and quiet menace.

'Take your…heavier clothes off…th-then

get into the base of the hedge and dig. The l-leaves will be warmer than the air and they will p-protect you.'

He made no attempt to move himself, the flakes of snow thicker now. Again red blood pooled beneath him.

She came to a decision without conscious thought. He had saved her twice and she could not leave him here to perish. Unbuttoning what was left of his shirt, she sat him forward and took away the sodden cotton. His jacket was long gone, probably discarded when he first went into the river. A chain hung at his neck, a ring secured upon it, white-gold with a large clear emerald.

Was he married? Did a woman wait at home for him, hoping? His eyes this close were ringed in dark blue, grey melting into the colour seamlessly. Watching her.

'Go.'

But she could not. Unsheathing the knife along the line of her lower arm as strength re-turned, she stood and cut a pile of branches. The leaves that lay at the base of a hedge she fashioned into a bed and rolled him into it, placing many more leaves and plant stems on top and using the brush as a shield to keep the snow away. Then, climbing underneath to join him, she snuggled in, jacket and shirt gone, skin touching skin.

Already the day had darkened, the dusk misting in early with the weather, more clouds on the horizon.

'Will they find us?'

'Not today. S-snow covers everything and whoever is looking will have to w-wait it out.'

Their small lair was becoming darker as the snow caught, layering and thickening. The wind, too, had lessened and heat was beginning to build. She liked it when his arms came about her, holding her close, the beat of his heart even and unhurried and his breath comforting.

For this one small moment they were safe.

She was glad when he stopped shivering, their warmth melding together to create hope.

Nat had awoken from their lair of snow beneath the bushes to a room with a fire burning bright. An older man and woman sat observing them, a youth standing near the window.

'Our dog found your tracks leading from the river and we brought you here early this morning.'

Looking about, he saw that Sandrine and he had been placed on a bed together, a thick feather down quilt across them. He knew immediately that they were both naked, for she was tucked about him as if in sleep her body had sought the warmth she so desperately needed.

'Your clothes and boots have been washed and repaired and should be dry by nightfall. The doctor said you were to stay very quiet for the wound at your side would have taken much in energy from you and could open again if you are not careful.'

A headache pounded in Nat's temples, impairing his vision, the room swimming as their words were lost into a droning noise. Sandrine was still asleep, their voices making no inroad into her consciousness.

Shaking his head, he tried to distil the blurriness, but the pain only intensified and so he desisted. He could not even move a muscle; a heavy stupor anchored him to the mattress, and a tiredness that defied description seeped through. Alarm furrowed his brow, but when the dark claimed him he no longer had the vigour to question it, demand it different.

Sandrine was awake before him when he

next surfaced and she had moved a good distance away, a rough linen shift now in place across her shoulders. A grey blanket was wedged in the space between them and no one else was in the room. A fire danced in the grate.

'Madame Dortignac has just left. She brought chicken broth if you want some.'

'No.' The thought of food turned his stomach. Outside it was pitch-black and the noises of the house were stilled. Late, then? Around two, perhaps, though he had no real measure of time.

'It has rained heavily all day,' Sandrine said after a moment, 'and I heard them say that the river has come up.'

'Good.' The threads of protection began to wind in closer. 'Any sign of our presence will be long gone from the mud on the banks.'

'They brought in a priest for you. I think they were worried you might not survive.'

'When?'

'Yesterday afternoon. It has been a full two days since you last awoke.' Anxiety played in her eyes. 'He asked if we were husband and wife before he left. When I said that we were not he was displeased.'

'A result of our bedding arrangements, I suspect. They think that I have ruined you.'

'The priest tried to make me go to another room, but I felt safe here and told him that I would not.'

She looked so damn young sitting there, the dark beneath her eyes worrying him and the homespun in her shift showing up the fragility of her shoulders. Her hair had been pulled back into a loose chignon, small curls escaping around her face. Feeling the punch of her beauty Nathaniel breathed out and glanced away, angry at the effect she so easily engendered on the masculine parts of his body, even in sickness. He could not remember any woman with such sway over him.

Safe?

If he had felt better, he might have laughed at her interpretation of security. Looking around for his sword and gun, he found them next to his carefully folded clean clothes and polished boots to one side of the bed.

'Did they say who they were?

She nodded. 'Farmers. They own the land between the river and the mountains behind, a large tract that has been in their family for generations. The Catholic priest who came was

certain that God was punishing us for…for….'
She did not finish.

He smiled. 'Our sins of the flesh?'

A bright stain of redness began at her throat
and surged up across her cheeks.

'Life or death requires sacrifices, Sandrine,
and if you had not removed my clothes and
kept me warm I would have perished. An om-
nipotent God would know that, and I thank
you for it.'

A myriad of small expressions flitted across
her brow: humour, puzzlement and then finally
acceptance.

'Are you always so certain of things, Monsieur Colbert?'

'Yes.'

At that she laughed properly, her head
thrown back and her eyes dancing. Not the
pale imitation of laughter that the society
ladies had perfected to an art form, but a real
and honest reaction that made him laugh, too,
the medicine of humour exhilarating. He could
not remember ever feeling like this with another woman before, the close edge of a genuine joy pressing in and a camaraderie that
was enticing.

But when he reached out to touch her fingers humour dissipated into another emotion altogether. Connection, if he might name it, or shock, the sear of her flesh burning up into the cold of his arm.

She had felt it, too—he could tell she had as she snatched her hand away and buried it into the heavy grey of the blanket. Her face was turned from his so deliberately that the corded muscle in her throat stood out with tension, a pulse beating with rhythm that belied calmness.

Nathanael Colbert was as beautiful as he was powerful and even with the fever flushing his cheeks and tearing into the strength of him he still offered her protection. Outside, the night clothed the land in silence and inside his warmth radiated towards her, the barrier of wool insubstantial.

If she had been braver, she might have reached over and removed it, so that their skin could touch again as it had done before, close and real, offering safety and something else entirely.

Urgency. Craving. A yearning that she had no experience of, but that was there in her flesh and bones, the call of something ancient and destined, an undeniable and inescapable knownness.

Shocking. Wonderful. She did not wish him to see the remnants of all she thought so she turned away, pleased when he did not demand her attention or reach out again.

An impasse in a cold and wind-filled night, the mountains of the Pyrenees filling a darkened sky and a fire measuring out the passing moments in warmth.

One and then two. Enough to regain composure and push away the thoughts of what might have been between them should they have given it a chance. An ache wormed its way across her throat and heart before settling lower. Loss could be a physical hurt, she would think much later, but right now it was a wondrous and startling surprise.

Chancing a look at him, she saw he lay back against the pillows, the sheet pulled away from the dark nakedness of his skin, muscle sculptured under the flame light. Still sick, she realised, by the sheen of sweat across his brow and the high colour in his cheeks. She wondered how the wound at his side had fared from such exertion, but did not dare to ask him, given the state of her racing heart.

'I will protect you, Sandrine. Do not worry.'
The words were quietly said.

'From everyone?'

His lips turned up, the dimple in his right
cheek deepening.

'Yes.'

She did not wipe away the tear that traced
down her face, but waited to feel the cold run
of its passage, the blot of moisture darkening the yellowed counterpane as it fell. As his
breathing evened out she knew he was asleep,
his body needing the balm of rest. Turning
with as little noise as possible, she watched
him, his breathing shallow and fast and his
dark eyelashes surprisingly long.

The past few days rushed up at her, the
chaos and the hope. Baudoin and his brother
had been bandits whose livelihood was made
by taking the riches from aristocrats travelling
the roads towards the north and west, but Guy
Lebansart was a different story altogether. He
boasted about working for the French Government, though Sandrine knew enough about
the houses and land that he had accrued to
know that more lucrative pickings had taken
his fancy.

Lebansart blackmailed people and he hurt

anyone who got in his way—even Anton Baudoin had been scared of him. He had been due to arrive at the compound with a good deal of gold in exchange for information found on a man Baudoin's men had killed on the highway. But Nathaniel Colbert had arrived first.

A coincidence.

Sandrine thought not.

Glancing again at the stranger, she frowned. What were his secrets? Closing her eyes, she fervently prayed that Lebansart and those who worked for him would never catch up with them.

Chapter Three

Cassandra smoothed down the wool of her pantaloons and pulled up the generous collar of her jacket. It was cold in the London wind and it had already begun to spit.

Damn, she cursed, for the sound of the rain would dull her hearing and she knew that dawn wasn't far off.

Lord Nathaniel Lindsay had returned to his town house a quarter of an hour ago, and by his gait as he descended from the carriage she knew he had been drinking.

Perfect.

The thick line of trees in the garden surprised her. She would not have imagined him to sanction such a shelter, for intruders could easily use the screen to hide behind. Making her way through the green-tinged darkness, she sidled along the undergrowth until she came to the windows.

The first sash was rock solid. The next one moved. Unsheathing her knife, she pressed it into the crack and shifted the lock. One second and it was rendered useless, clicking into access. With an intake of breath she lifted the wood, and when she perceived no threat she raised it farther.

Waiting, she listened to the sounds of the room. A single last fall of wood in the grate as the warm air greeted her, a clock in the corner marking out the hour.

She was over the barrier in a whisper, turning to the chamber and waiting as her eyes accustomed themselves.

'Shut the window and join me.'

He knew she would come for he had seen a shadow that was not normally there against the stone wall on the opposite side of the street. This window had always been loose, a trick of wet wood or poor craftsmanship, he knew not which.

To give her credit she barely acknowledged the shock. A slight hesitation, one less certain step. He wondered if she held a knife in her hand and thought perhaps he should have bothered to arm himself. But he would not have harmed her. He knew that without a doubt.

'Lord Nathaniel Lindsay, the heir to the title of St Auburn?' Her voice was tight, tinged with more than a hint of question.

'At your service, Mademoiselle Mercier. And now you are all grown up.'

'A fact that you hate?'

He laughed at that because her surprising honesty had always appealed to him, though the sound held little humour. 'I survived, but others did not. The names I presume you gave to Lebansart made it easy for him to mark them off as English agents. Didier and Gilbert Desrosiers were like lambs to the slaughter. Good men. Men who had never wronged you in any way. Men with allegiances to England and who had only ever wanted to serve this country.'

The blood seemed to disappear from her face. One moment her cheeks were rosy from the outside cold and in the next second they were as pale as snow.

'You were a spy, too? My God, that explains why you were there in France and in Nay in particular.'

'They call them intelligence officers now.'

'You were a spy for the English army?'

'The British Service.'

'Not just the army then, but the quiet and hidden corridors of a clandestine and covert agency. Are you still?'

He did not answer.

'I will take that as a yes, then.' The blood had returned to her face, and she did not waver as she went on. 'I didn't come to offer excuses for what I did at Perpignan, my lord, nor for exoneration.'

'Then why did you come?'

'To give you this.'

She took a ring from her pocket and he recognised it immediately. His mother's, the emerald as green as it had been all those years before.

'I took it and I should not have. For all the other things that I was, I was never a thief.'

'God.' Thief of hearts, he thought. Thief of lives. Thief of the futures of two good Englishmen caught in the crossfire of politics.

'Celeste died for nothing. At least those agents of England that you speak of perished for a cause they believed in. A righteous cause.

A cause to take them into Heaven and be pardoned by our Lord for it.'

'You came tonight to tell me this?' His voice shook with bitterness.

'No. I came to say that nothing is as black and as white as it seems, and the documents I saw were there for others to see as well.'

'Yet you memorised them and gave the information back to the one person you should not have.'

'Guy Lebansart was only one man who might have wanted them dead. France was seething with those who would harm anyone with loyalties to England. Perhaps they held your name, too?'

'I doubt I was on any index of names.'

'Then you doubt wrong,' she said and turned to the window. 'From the moment you rescued me there was danger.'

And then he understood. 'So you traded our freedom for intelligence? Hell.' So many questions and so few answers. Yet something was not quite right. And then the penny dropped.

'I was the one you bargained for?'

The nod she gave him was almost imperceptible. 'Indeed, that was a part of the story, but now I need a favour, Lord Lindsay. I need the right to go on with my life without having to look behind at the chaos, waiting for it to catch up.'

'And nothing else?'

'Nothing.'

Her voice was measured. No extra emotion. No telltale sign of weakness or feeling. She had sacrificed the lives of others for his and she knew there was no honour in any of it. It was not thanks she had come for. Neither was it a penance. Celeste was probably more of a part of it than anyone, for Sandrine had always been like a mother lioness over any perceived tarnishing of her cousin's memory and she might have been fearful about the recount of his knowledge of her.

The complex layers of guilt and shame mixed in strangely with integrity. She had not needed to come. He hadn't further want for the ring and no explanation could absolve murder.

'You whored in exchange for my life?'

She shook away the words. 'You know nothing, Colbert.'

'Lindsay,' he corrected her with a cold and hard fury.

'If I had not traded the information, you would have been dead.'

'And instead…?'

'You lived.'

Her eyes flickered to the scar that ran across his jaw on the right side.

'Death might have been kinder.'

She raised her fist at that, the hand of ruined and knotted skin. 'You think I did not wish that, too, many times after I left you, the blood of those I'd named wrapped about the heart of my guilt? But there is no book written on the rules of war, my lord, and I was a young girl trying to exist in a world that had forsaken me. Anton Baudoin had taken the documents from a man he had murdered a few days before you came to Nay. I had no idea as to who those mentioned within it were.'

Silence filled the space between them for the time it took the clock in the corner to chime out the hour of two. It was why he had come to find the Baudoins in the first place, pointed in the direction by intelligence garnered after the agent's murder. Then she spoke again.

'You think I should have trusted you enough to make a run for it at Perpignan and believed that the impossible might be probable there with a hundred enemies at our heels and many more behind? You believed in that option of faith?'

'Yes.' Simple. Heartfelt.

Her unexpected smile was a sad one. 'On reflection you may have been correct because what happened afterwards took away all my right of choice.' There was a new note in her words now. Resignation and acceptance mixed with an undercurrent of shame.

'Merde.' The French word echoed through the dark like a gunshot. One moment a history just guessed at and the next known exactly.

'But I have made a new life here, a good life, a life that helps those whom all others have forgotten.'

'The Daughters of the Poor?'

She nodded, but in the depths of her eyes he saw the truth of what they had each found out about the other shimmering. Unspoken. The lump in his throat hitched in memory and it rested in the spaces after midnight, the weight of such knowledge making him turn away, pain lapping at all they could never say.

'I help ruined girls like me.'

He hated that pretence was no longer possible.

'Get out.' Usually he was more urbane and polished, but with her he had never been quite himself.

'Not until you agree to what I have asked.'

He did not speak because he did not trust in what he might say, but when he nodded she was gone, the whisper of the velvet curtains as they fell against the sash and a faint eddy of wind. Placing his head against the wall, he closed his eyes and cursed.

No one can get back what is lost.

That is what she had whispered then, that last time, as she had untwined his shaking fingers from around her wrist and gone with the French spymaster, her laughter on the air as rough hands wormed into the young promise of girlhood.

The sacking shield had come down as her footsteps receded, the twine it was held in place with tight at his throat. He remembered the sharp blade of a knife pressed into his ribs just below his heart.

'Sandrine, the whore.' Someone had drawled the words behind him as he had been pushed into midair and then he could remember nothing.

* * *

Cassandra was shaking so much she could barely untie her trousers and unbuckle her boots. Two good men had died because of her disclosure and Nathaniel Lindsay hated her now as easily as she had loved him, then. A young girl of shattered dreams and endless guilt. The hero in Nathanael Colbert had beckoned like a flame and she had been burnt to a cinder.

She was so utterly aware of Lindsay; that was the problem. Even now, safe in her room, the thrum of her want for him made her body vibrate. She forced stillness and crossed to the mirror above the hearth, its rim of gold leaf scratched by age. The woman who stared back was not the one she felt inside. This woman still held on to promise and hope, her eyes dancing with passion, heated skin sending rose into pale cheeks.

He had no reason to assent to all that she asked, no obligation to the betrayal and deceit lingering beyond the limits of honour. And yet he had assented.

She thrust her hand instinctively against one breast and squeezed it hard. No joy in this, no pleasure. No reward of the flesh, but the broken promises of men.

Turning away, she swallowed, the anger of her life forming strength. It was all she had, all she could hold on to. Once, other oaths had held her spellbound in the safety of Celeste's bedroom in Perpignan, and under the light of a candle that threw the flame of curiosity on to two young faces.

'Papa said that we can all go to Barages. It has been so long since we have been anywhere, Sandrine, and taking in the waters would be something we can all enjoy.'

'Will David come, too?'

'If you are going he is bound to want to for I have seen the way my father's godson looks at you. But be warned, although he is eighteen he is also far too boring.'

Cassie blushed, hating the red that often rose in her cheeks at the mention of anything personal. She had arrived in France four months earlier, travelling from London by boat into Marseilles in the company of her mother's brother and her cousin, and the warmth of the south had seeped into her bones like a tonic.

'I want to meet someone who will take my breath away. A rich man, a good-looking man, a dangerous man.' Celeste's voice held that thread of wishfulness that Cassandra had often heard her use. 'I am so very tired of the milksop sons of my father's friends.'

'But what of Jules Durand?' Her cousin's latest swain had been at the door most days, professing his love and his intentions, a strange mix of shyness and gall.

'He is not…manly enough. He tells me too much before I want him to. He kissed my hand yesterday and all I could think of was to pull away from the wet limpness of his lips.'

All of a sudden the conversation had gone to places Cassandra did not understand, the edge of virtue tarnished by a feeling that seemed… bruised. Celeste had grown up in the year since she had seen her, the lines of her body curvy and fuller. Tonight under the bedcovers some other feeling lingered, something wrong and false.

Her cousin's blue eyes flashed. 'Do you never wish for a man's hands upon your body, finding the places that feel only magic? Do you not want to know the wonderment that all the great books talk of?'

'No.' Cassie pulled the collar of her nightgown full around her throat. Her own bedroom

was down the corridor amongst the shadows
and she had been scared to stay there, but this
room suddenly held a fear that she could not
comprehend.

'You are no longer in boring stuffy old England. Here women know the dance of love and
they flaunt it.' Rising from her bed, Celeste
simply pulled off her gown, standing against
the flame of her lamp like a goddess.

'I want to know what it is to be passionate
and wanton and brave. Only dull wits shall be
for ever stuck with one boring husband for the
rest of their lives and I certainly shall not be
that. When we are young we should be able to
know…everything.'

Cassie's eyes ran across the fat abundance
of her cousin's breasts, breasts that were so
different from her own. Celeste's waist had
slimmed and her hips had spread and the hair
between her legs had been trimmed back into
the shape of a heart.

'You look beautiful.' The words came from
the very depth of admiration.

'Too beautiful to be wasted on the boys
that I am forever annoyed by here.' One hand
cupped her breast and the other fell to the soft
place between her legs. 'There is no power

more durable than that of womanhood. No influence over men as strong as the desire for sex. Remember that, Cassandra, when you do finally grow up, and use it wisely.'

Draping a blanket around herself then, she smiled, turning again into the more-known cousin, the girl who would push the boundaries, but was kinder with it.

'You look shocked, Sandrine.' She began to laugh in earnest now. 'Shocked and stiff. I do not think you are made for such confessions.'

All the words fell across Cassandra. Words she had not heard before or thought of. Ideas that had been a part of a world far from her own, lost in the corruption of love. She wished she were home in England, Maureen in the chamber next door and her father not far away either. Rodney was too young to think much of right now, but even his presence would have been a relief.

'Come, let us sleep, cousin, and I promise I shall behave myself entirely. You have been ill, after all, and I should not tease you.'

In her bedroom in London all those years later Cassandra dashed away the tears that came so readily whenever she thought of Celeste. Her cousin's promise had been fulfilled in blood and in pain, the danger of Baudoin's brother Louis and the wildness within him no match for a slightly wayward French virgin steeped in the potential of adventure and romance.

'Romance.' She whispered the word into the room, and it curled into sin. Some losses were beyond comprehension and this was one of those. Some truths, too, were made mute by their sheer and utter horror.

Her truths.

No, she could never let Lord Nathaniel Lindsay know the exact depth of any of them and after discovering today that he worked for the British Service she knew she would have to be more than careful. Just another gulf of difference between them that could never be bridged.

Lady Acacia Bellowes-Browne hung on to his arm at the Smithson ball and laughed, a soft musical sound that ran through tenseness and made Nathaniel relax.

'You said that you would come down to Bellamy for the hunting, Nat. I have held that promise for some weeks now'

'And indeed I shall,' he answered, liking the feel of her fingers on his skin, the many rings she wore decorative and colourful. He was about to speak again when Lydia Forsythe came across to the group.

'I am sorry to disturb you, Lord Lindsay, but I want to thank you for your help the other week. Mama said you were most kind in ensuring that I did not bleed to death.'

'I rather think that you would not have.'

'Well, Miss Cassandra Northrup said that I might and she is thought to be most proficient of all in the arts of medicine. When I visited her to give her my thanks she barely allowed my gratitude. Instead, she has asked for my help with her charity. Mama, of course, does not approve, but I think it is important…to remember about the plight of others, I mean…' She petered off as Acacia began to speak.

'Cassandra Northrup has lobbied us all in her pursuit of supporting those less fortunate.'

Interest sparked his question. 'You think she is too assertive in her search for patrons?'

'No, not that. She is known to delve into the shady corners of London when locating all the broken women and I think she understands neither the dangers nor the gossip associated with such an occupation. She looks as if butter would not melt in her mouth, but I have it on all accounts that she is well versed in the art of self-defence.'

'Isn't she just wonderful?' Lydia Forsythe's eyes were alight with hero worship, and the woman standing with Hawk, who Nat had not met before, also nodded her head.

A paragon and model of charitable benevolence. What would these people say if they were cognizant of the truth as he knew it? He had not told a soul about the names she had given to Lebansart. A questionable protection? A foolish guardianship? Even for England he had not betrayed her.

'She will never marry again, of course. She has made that quite plain.' Acacia's voice drifted into his thoughts.

'She won't?'

'No, my lord. The love of her life was lost in a terrible accident in Paris and she has no want to ever offer her heart to another.'

Nat's mind scrambled. Paris?

'Well, I think that it is romantic to tender thoughts for a husband long dead.' Lydia Forsythe for all her youth was most outspoken in her opinions. 'I have asked the Northrup sisters to my ball and they have promised to attend.'

'An inducement of money for the cause would no doubt bring them running,' Acacia was quick to add. 'The Daughters of the Poor is a worthwhile charity, however. I have a maid acquired from that very organisation and she has been a godsend. Cassandra Northrup's benevolent society is both efficient and organised.'

'She has a school somewhere?' Nathaniel could not believe what he was hearing.

'In Holborn. When the girl was sent to me she was well equipped with clothes and books. Miss Maureen Northrup is apparently the one who sees to that side of the business.'

Hawk began to laugh. 'They sound formidable.'

'They are. Kenyon Riley is involved in the endeavour as well.'

'I thought he had lost a leg somewhere in America?'

'Lost a leg and gained a fortune.' Hawk took up the conversation. 'And his great-uncle, the old Duke, is about to die without issue.'

'A timely inheritance, then, for the Northrups.'

'Oh, indeed,' Acacia trilled. 'And Kenyon is most besotted by them.'

Nat looked away. Cassandra Northrup had a knack of landing on her feet after adversity and using others to the very best of her own advantage.

Of all the men in the world he was the one to know that.

'Maureen Northrup has her own worries.' A wide frown marred Acacia's brow.

Now this was new.

'She does?'

'She is virtually deaf. She lip-reads, of course, and speaks in her inimitable fashion, but it is the younger sister who runs the show.'

'And the father?'

'Lord Cowper is a man who has tried to carry on the life's work of his beloved wife. Something of tiny animals we cannot see that live on our skin and make us sick.'

Nathaniel's mind went back. Sandrine had insisted upon dousing his gunshot wound in the clearing all those years ago with water and she had cleaned her hands before she had touched him. She believed in these things, too, then. Every single fact he heard about her was more astonishing than the last.

'I have read of this. Such a hypothesis is gaining in traction in scientific circles as a credible theory.'

Acacia spread out her fingers and peered at them against the light. 'Well, I can see no sign of these things of which they speak and because of the wild claims of their science there are many here in society who do not view the Northrups with much kindness. Bluestockings frighten men of little brain.'

Hawk began to laugh loudly. 'Not quite the ideal of Victorian expectation.'

'By virtue of ornamental innocence, you mean?' Acacia shook her head as she said it.

Innocence.

The word stretched across the years, and Nathaniel was back beside the river in the small cottage of the Dortignacs, his new wife's hair spilled across the pillow like living streams of fire and gold.

Madam and Monsieur Dortignac had insisted they both be up the next morning, bathed and dressed in clothes that were remarkably formal. It was therefore no surprise when a man of the cloth had appeared an hour later, although the blood had ebbed from Sandrine's cheeks as she had grasped the intention of his visit.

'Marriage? They want us to be married now?'

'They feel as though they have fallen from grace, so to speak, by allowing us the freedoms of sharing a bed. This is their way of making amends with God.'

'But you cannot possibly want this?'

He smiled. The light caught at her hair this morning and tumbled across the soft green-blue of her eyes. 'Sometimes when people need things with as much passion as they need us to marry it does not hurt to humour them. Particularly given that they saved our lives by their actions and probably put their own at risk.'

'You think it wise, then?'

'I do.'

'Well, I should never hold you to such a farce, Monsieur Colbert,' Sandrine said. 'If we are wed by simple expedience and obligation then who should need to know of it when we leave here?'

God. You. Me. The priest. Two names in a book that make this union traceable? Nat said none of what he thought, however, as he looped the chain over his head and unhooked the clasp.

'I received this after my mother died. It belonged to her mother and her grandmother before that.'

'Then you shouldn't risk it with me.'

Ignoring her protest, he lifted her left hand, the cold smallness of it within his warmth. 'Let's try it for size.'

It did not fit her ring finger, but it nearly held on her middle one. When they reached Perpignan he would have it resized.

'It almost looks as though it could be a real emerald,' she said quietly, and he smiled as the Dortignacs and the priest came into their room. Madam Dortignac had found some winter wild flowers and she handed the straggly bouquet to Sandrine with a smile.

'For you, my dear, she said softly. 'The very last of the autumn purple crocuses.'

Much later, as Sandrine held her arm out so that the light glinted upon his mother's ring, it was impossible to clarify what he felt, the witchery of the sickness from the wound at his side still holding him prisoner, yet something else free and different.

But while his mind was ambiguous, Nat's body was not and the need in him surfaced beneath thin sheets. She had felt it, too, he thought, because she rolled over to watch him, a silent, wary question in her eyes and a hint of compliance. Her lips turned up at each end like the beginnings of a smile, a girl changing into woman right before his very eyes.

He could not help his want, nor could he rein in all that was left better unseen, the words of troth between them allowing whatever it was they might desire: warmth, relief, resolution.

Or nothing, with their sickness.

He wished he might touch her in quiet acquiescence, but instead he turned onto his back, sense winning out.

'They were more than happy to leave us alone this time.'

At that she laughed, joy enveloped in the dark closeness.

He remembered the feel of her in the bed when he had awoken that first time, the contours of her body, the thinness, the elegance. Like catching energy and holding it.

'You were a beautiful bride, Sandrine Mercier, with your hair let down.'

'And my bare feet. Don't forget those. But I think green suited me.'

'Indeed. The ancient gown was particularly flattering.'

'It was our hostess's grandmother's and it was twenty sizes too large. At least you had clothes that fitted.'

He held his tongue and wished that they were home at St Auburn, the English winter about them and everything familiar. When she had taken off the wedding gown after the ceremony the lines of her ribs had been drawn starkly on her skin.

'You are too thin.' He should not have said the words, he knew, a piece of paper gave him no mandate for such a criticism, but it was concern that made him speak, not disparagement.

'I was sick. For a long time.'

'At Nay?'

'Before that even.'

'And now?'

She shrugged and looked directly at him. 'Have you ever lost someone close to you?'

He looked away.

'My whole family, apart from my grandfather.' He wondered at what had made him say it, made him confess to a hurt he had always held so very far from others.

Her fingers crawled into his, warm and true,

the honesty of the connection endearing. He coughed to clear the thickness in his throat and thought with all this emotion he must be more ill than he knew.

'My own mama died fifteen months ago. It was an accident.'

She stressed the last word in an odd manner, making Nat wonder if perhaps it wasn't.

'I was there when it happened and the doctor thinks my mind became damaged. Afterwards I could not be…happy. Papa grew impatient and I was sent on the journey south with my mother's brother and his daughter to recuperate and forget.'

Cassie swallowed and held on to him even more tightly. The fever made her head swim and her vision blurry, but she knew exactly what she was saying. She needed to tell him— there was no going back because in the past few days even under the duress of hiding from those who would want to find them she had suddenly felt free. At liberty to be honest and say all that had been held bound in her mind.

'It was my fault.'

He did not even flinch. 'The accident?'

'I added some liquid to her experiment before she had asked for it to be done and the vapour from it made her sick right then and there. She died three hours later.'

'How old were you?'

'Sixteen. Old enough to wait and listen.'

'The exactness of science is sometimes over-exaggerated and the emotion of blame is the same.'

His voice was quiet, unfazed. For the first time in a long while Cassie did not feel breathless.

'Did you intend to kill her?' he asked finally.

'Of course not.' Shock jagged through her.

'But you knew that those particular elements combined might cause a problem?'

'No. I have no true understanding of all the properties of things.'

Dropping her fingers, he stretched his arms above his head, linking them under his neck so that he could watch her with more ease.

'Once, when I was small, I took a horse and rode it for hours until the steed sat down and died. My father said the horse could have stopped running with my light and small touch upon it, or thrown me off into the brush. He said the stallion did neither because he wanted to keep running. His choice. Would your mother have added the next ingredient of her experiment if you had not been there?'

'I think so.'

'Then it was her choice.'

'But I ruined our family. Papa told me so.'

'No. I think if your father blamed you, it was he who did that completely by himself.'

Perception. Skewered into truth. It was all she could do to stop the tears of a relief that felt indescribable. Someone else believed that she was not responsible even with all the facts at hand. More of the inheld tension that she always felt melted away.

Colbert had saved her in the river, she knew, the water in her throat and in her eyes, the heavy panic of exhaustion pulling her down. He had saved her, too, when he had insisted on the hole covered in leaves and branches being made on the leeward side of the bush, tucked into calm. How would she have found shelter otherwise without his knowledge of survival?

Survival was marked on his skin, in the scars of bullet and knife. On the upper side of his fighting arm she saw the blue mark of indigo. A serpent curled about a stake.

A man who had lived a hundred hard lives and come through each one. She needed this certainty and this prowess because for the first time in years hope inside began to beat again.

Not all ruined. Not all lost.

A small refrain of promise.

When she smiled at him he smiled back and Cassie felt, quite suddenly, reborn. 'How old are you?'

'Twenty-three.' He added the word *ancient* in a whisper.

'Yet you haven't married?'

'I've been busy.'

The stillness in him magnified. He never fussed, she thought, or used up energy in movements that were surplus. For a big man there was a sense of grace about him that made one look again and wonder. The danger of a panther about to strike, the liquid stretch of muscle honed with a precision that was undeniable, jeopardy tethered to a strict and unrelenting accuracy.

She had seen it in Nay in the way he fought and again at the barn by the river. Someone had trained him well. The government or an army? No amateur could have forged such expertise, but a political mercenary might have managed it. Once a man similar to Colbert had come to Baudoin's compound in the company of a French General, and had been accorded much respect and esteem.

This was Nathanael Colbert's legacy, too. No one could look at him and fail to see the menace, even when he was sick almost to death and the fever burned. Glancing away, she felt her stomach clench. To have someone like this on her side...

She shook the thought gone. One day if she was lucky she would remember back at this moment and know that just for a small time he had been hers, her husband, a ring on her finger and the simmering potential of more. She wished her body had had the curves of Celeste and that she might have met him in Paris as a woman of an impeccable reputation and virtue. They could have danced then to a waltz perhaps, her dress of spun gold matching her hair and at her throat her mother's diamonds. She could have flirted with him, held her fan in that particular way of a coquette and watched him through smoky eyes, the promise of all that might happen between them so very possible.

And instead? Her ruined hand on the counterpane caught her attention, the missing part of her forefinger and the long red scar easy to see in the moonlight.

'Could you kiss me?'

Her words were out, an entreaty in them that she had tried so hard to hide. But the emotion of the day was thrumming underneath everything they said and if she parted company with him, as she knew she would, she did not want to be left forever wondering. Or wishing.

For a moment she thought he had not heard or had not wanted to hear and her fists clenched by her side. But then he moved, balancing on his arm and leaning across her, his eyes the grey of the sea at dawn just after the sunrise.

Nathanael's lips were as she had imagined they might be, soft at first and then harder, searching for things that held a promise. Gentle and strong, harnessed by both power and care, his free hand caressing the line of her neck and bringing her closer.

Only them in the world, only this, she thought, as she rose up to him, her tongue meeting his and tasting. She allowed him to force her back against the pillow, the darkness behind her closed eyes calling for more. She felt him turn and come across her body, the outline of his chest meeting her breasts, though his elbows kept the bulk of his body away. The shiver of passion, the heat of want, the memory of this day quickening as he covered her mouth and kept her breath as his own.

A wife and her husband.

Then he broke away. 'When I am not so sick, Sandrine, I promise to take the kiss much, much further.'

Under the cover of darkness Cassie smiled because his heart was racing every bit as much as hers and when he turned away as if to quell all the thoughts his body was consumed by, she simply curled up into his warmth.

But it was a long, long while until she finally went to sleep.

They woke to the crow of a rooster outside, and inside Cassie could hear the movements of the Dortignacs preparing for a new day, the dawn only a little while off.

'We will leave with the first light,' he said as if he had been listening too. 'If Baudoin's henchmen following us find these people have been sheltering us...' There was no need for him to finish.

To the south, the mountains of the Pyrenees seemed to hold their breath, dark with the presage of rain. Another cold day. A further freezing trek towards Perpignan, many long and difficult miles to the east.

When Nathanael sat up on the side of the bed she saw the bandage across his wound was sagging. She should change it, she knew, but she did not think he would allow it and so she did not say. When he put on his clothes she understood he was in a hurry to leave and that the quiet moments of honesty between them had come to an end.

He looked healthier today. She could see it in the way he stood, no longer favouring his right side in the way he was yesterday. She also saw in his expression a hint of the promise he had made after kissing her.

In the new day, Cassie suddenly understood the danger of a relationship. She needed to go on alone from here because she was certain Lebansart and his men could not be far behind, and if Nathanael died for her...

She shook her head.

If she struck out early across the hills, she could find a pathway and other travellers and make her way to any larger town in the vicinity.

Monsieur and Madam Colbert.

For one night of marriage only.

He had saved her so many times it was only right that she must now protect him.

Chapter Four

Cassandra came across the rooftops in darkness and down into the interior of the brothel on Brown Street without being seen by anybody. An easy climb given the footholds and the balconies, but on gaining the room the note had instructed her to come to she could tell that something was wrong. Very wrong.

The chamber door was wide open and the man Cassandra had been looking for was already dead on the floor by the window. Crossing to the glass, she tested the locks, but rust inside the catches told her nobody had come this way. With care, she dropped to her knees and checked beneath the bed, knife in hand and ready to strike. Only the empty space of blackness.

She was glad for the silence in the room

for it gave her a moment to think. He had not taken off any of his clothes. There had been no struggle at all and he was unmarked save for the wound at his neck. Money still lay in his pockets when she checked and an expensive leather briefcase languished in full view beside the doorway.

His right arm was bandaged, the thickness of the casing beneath his jacket belying the injury. His other arm was positioned above his head, the gold ring on his finger seen in the light.

Not a robbery then. Not a targeted wealthy man who had come to the wrong place at the wrong time and run into one of the shady characters off Whitechapel Road. Someone he knew had done this, a strike from behind without a notion that it was about to happen.

Walking to the bed, she took the bag and flicked open the buckles. Surprise made her eyes widen. Nothing lay inside, every pocket emptied and all the compartments clean. The perpetrator had been after this then, the contents of the satchel, and for such information had been willing to kill. Loud shouting made her stiffen, the sound of boots coming up the steep stairwell and voices in the night.

With only a whisper of noise she crossed from the room to the doorway and let herself out. She couldn't be found like this—in the garb of a street boy with a weapon in her belt—and she did not have the time in hand to make it up the next flight of stairs to safety without being noticed. With care she picked the lock of the room opposite and eased herself through the door. No one was in the bed and for that she was more than thankful. Dulling the noise of the closing door with the cloth in her jacket, she jimmied her foot up against the wood and flipped the latch.

Nat did not move a muscle from the alcove he stood in by the window, his breath shallow. Outside the noises were getting louder and inside the intruder stayed immobile. Was the newcomer a child? A youth of the house, perhaps, trying to escape the nefarious pursuits as best he could? The glint of a knife told him otherwise and he was across the room before the other knew it, his hand hitting out at the arm that was raised and knocking the weapon away.

He knew it was Cassandra Northrup even before she turned, the scent and the feel of her, the knowledge of each other burning bright. Bringing her against him, he felt the lines of her body even as she fought him, the fuller contours unfamiliar.

'Stop, Sandrine.' Whispered. Danger was everywhere and the discovery of a lady within the confines of such iniquity would be scandalous. Her breath was ragged, the warmth of it against his hand where he held it flat across her mouth.

She stilled, as much to listen to the noises outside the door as to obey him, her head tipped to the wood, jumping as a heavy knock sounded against it.

'Don't open it. A man is dead and I cannot be found like this.' Whispered and frightened behind his fingers, the quicksilver change into a woman startling.

'Hell.' He let her go. She filled out the boy's clothes much more generously these days, though the thinness was still there, too.

'Take everything off and get under the covers.' Already he was peeling away his own clothes, throwing each piece against a chair. Randomly. Trying to give the impression of haste and passion mixed in a room that was conducive to neither.

'Sex,' he said as he saw she was not moving. 'This place expects it.'

He pulled one dusty quilt off the bed and hung it over the other chair, hopeful in hiding the fact that female attire was missing. On a quick glance an observant onlooker would imagine them beneath.

'Open up.' A voice of authority. Probably the law.

It was enough to make her decide as her fingers flew to the buttons of her jacket and shirt, the lawn chemise beneath left on as she added her boots to the pile of clothes.

He brought those beneath the sheets with them, her body underneath his, concealed. He heard her gasp as the door opened, the correct key finally fitting the lock and giving way.

'What the hell…?' He barely needed to feign the anger as he looked around, two men in the uniform of the constabulary and the woman he had seen downstairs accompanying them. 'Get out, immediately.' He made himself sound breathless, the full blush of ardour in the words, a client in the middle of a 'paid for' assignation and surprised by the interruption. He also used his most aristocratic tones, the persona of a simple fellow disappearing into expediency. And carefully he shielded her from view.

He knew he had them as they faltered, a rush of apology. 'I am sorry, sir, but there has been a murder just reported in the house. If you could get dressed and come downstairs, we need to ask you some questions.'

Releasing a long rush of air, Nat nodded. 'Give me a few minutes and I shall be down.' No entreaty in it. Just authority.

The door closed behind them.

Silence.

Warmth.

Her skin against his own.

And then a curse. In French.

He pulled away and stood, making no attempt at hiding his body. 'Did you kill him?'

'No.'

'But you know who did?'

She shook her head.

'God.'

'Why did you help me?'

'Misguided instinct, though I am certain I shall now pay for such kindness. Is there a way out of here that does not involve going downstairs?' He reached for his clothes and began to dress.

'Yes.'

'Then I would advise you to take it.'

Already she was up, her shirt and jacket quickly donned, the boots following.

'I will expect you tomorrow.'

'Pardon?'

'At eleven p.m. Through the window of my town house to explain all this to me. Properly.'

'And if I refuse?'

'Then I will come to see you instead.'

'I will be there.'

'I thought so.'

'Will you be able to manage…everything?'

'Easily.'

She smiled. 'I always liked your certainty, Monsieur Nathanael Colbert.'

The music inherent in the way she said his name made him stiffen, and then she was gone.

His indiscretion was all over the town by midday, a lord of the first water visiting a brothel in the back streets of one of the worst areas of London and being caught out in doing so.

'You should have sent for me to come with you, Nat,' Stephen said as they sat in his library drinking brandy. 'Why the hell did you think to go there in the first place?'

'A man whom the prostitutes thought was acting strangely had been seen in the vicinity for each of the last two nights. They said he had slept at the brothel and was tall and well to do.'

'Was the dead man our murderer at the river, then?'

'No. He was short and stocky with ginger hair.'

'Memorable.'

'Exactly.'

Hawk suddenly smiled and leaned forward. 'There is something else I am missing here, Nat. It's the youngest Northrup daughter, isn't it? She was there at Whitechapel with you?'

Nathaniel ignored the query.

'The man killed at Brown Street last night was in the room opposite to mine and I heard nothing.'

'You paid for a room?'

'With a wide view of the street below. If the same man the girls spoke of was there, I would have seen him, Hawk, but I didn't.'

'Do you think the murder was related to our case?'

'Perhaps. The contents of the dead man's satchel was missing, though I found this in the corridor on my way down the stairs.' He dug into his pocket and brought out a single page of writing. 'Do you recognise the hand?'

Stephen looked carefully and then shook his head. 'Do you? It's a list for things from a chemist by the looks of it.'

'If I did, this case would already be half-solved. Will you do something for me, Hawk? Can you ask around to see if anyone saw anything? I do not want to seem interested because…'

'Because implication is only one step away from imprisonment and Cassandra Northrup's presence at Whitechapel will make everything that much harder again. Society does not seem exactly enamoured by her pursuit of the nefarious and a woman like that will only bring the old Earl's wrath down upon your head with even more than the usual vigour.'

'Remember that puppy we had at school, Hawk, the one we hid for a term in the wood-cutter's shed, the one you found off the road-side on the way to Eton?'

'Springer. My God, he was the best dog I ever owned.'

'Sixteen weeks of sneaking out twice a day with the food we had saved from the dining hall and then another jaunt for exercise. One hundred and twelve days before you could bundle him up and take him back to Atherton.'

'An unfortunate start to life, but he had the heart of a warrior till the day he died. But what is your point, Nat?'

'Cassandra Northrup is a fighter just like that dog and for some damned reason I feel compelled to help her.'

'You said she had betrayed you in France.'

'So did Springer. He bit you, remember, that time at the cliff….'

'Whilst trying to save me from falling.'

Nat drew his hand through his hair and wiped back the length of his fringe. 'What if Cassandra Northrup once did the same for me, Hawk? What if what she said she did and what she really did were two different things?'

'You are saying she might have betrayed you to save you?'

'I am.'

Cassandra had dressed carefully in a dark jacket and loose trousers, the cap she wore covering her face and her hair knotted in a bun at the back of her nape.

A caricature of Nathaniel Lindsay had appeared in the evening edition of a popular London broadsheet, one hand clinging on to the family crest and the other around the shapely ankle of a woman of the night. A poxed and toothless woman, her cheeks sunken with the mercury cure and rats scurrying from beneath the hem of her ragged skirt.

Lord Lindsay could not have been pleased; she knew this without listening to any gossip. He had also remained quiet about her involvement in this whole chaotic and sordid affair which, given the history between them, was a lot more than she might have expected.

Why he had been there in the first place she had no notion of, but he had been alone in the room waiting and completely dressed and when he had first pressed her against the door she had felt the outline of both knife and pistol.

Another thought also came. She had imagined she had been followed when she came to the boarding house in the backstreets of Whitechapel. Could it have been Lindsay watching?

The web of lies that bound them to each another was closing in, sticky with deceit, and yet here she was again, moving through his garden for a further encounter in his library. If she had any sense at all, she should be turning for home and ignoring his threats or packing her things and moving north for a while until the shock of seeing him again eased down into reason.

But she could not. Every fibre of her being could not.

He was exactly where he had been last time as she climbed through the window, his long legs out in front of the wing chair by the fire.

The only difference this time was that he had catered for her arrival, two glasses filled beside him.

'I have had a trying day,' he said as he handed one to her, 'and as you are the reason for it I hope you will join me in a drink.'

'A celebration of your notoriety?' Even as she gave the reply she wished she had not, but he only smiled.

'Yesterday the débutantes and their mothers were pursuing me with all the wiles in the world. Today they are…fleeing.'

'Sexual deviance may appear rather daunting to any woman, no matter the size of the purse an ancient family brings.'

At that he did laugh.

'How did you know the man who was murdered?'

'I didn't.'

'Then why were you there?'

'I had word of young girls being brought in from the country.'

'And you were attempting to locate them?' Lifting his glass, he held it up and waited for her to take a sip. Cassandra hated strong drink, but, not wishing to annoy him further, she took a mouthful and swallowed. The burning bitterness reminded her of Nay and of all that she longed to forget.

'The information I received gave a location, a time and a date, but when I got there the man was already dead.'

'With a knife in the back of his neck?'

'Yes.' She did not blink.

'What else did you see?'

'A briefcase that was empty of papers.'

'Papers like this one I found in the corridor outside the murdered man's room.'

He brought out a sheet of tightly written words. He knew she recognised it by her sudden stillness. 'Your father pens articles for a science journal. The editor is a friend of mine and I spent a few hours this afternoon with him. When, by chance, he showed me Lord Cowper's latest offering the two hands appeared identical.'

'That is what the person who put this there wanted you to think, wanted the constabulary to think. My father is the one person who can stop them.'

'How?'

'He funds the Daughters of the Poor, and we are making good progress in catching those who trade the lives of young girls for work in the factories and the brothels.'

'We, meaning you. You in your boy's clothes in the dead of night risking life, limb and reputation.'

'Gone.'

'Pardon?'

'My reputation is gone. You of all people should know that.'

'The redemption of a sinner then, brazen and unmindful. I expected more of you.'

'Oh, I have ceased trying to live up to any expectations save that of my own, my lord. Now prudence rules over heroics, which in itself is a timely lesson for all who might rally against injustice.'

'Society holds you up as a saint?'

'Hardly that.'

'But not as a whore?'

The quick punch of hurt and then nothing. By the time she had come out from that hovel of a building in Perpignan Nathanael Colbert had long been gone and she had wiped all trace of sacrifice from her conscience since.

Just a small space of hours, blurred by pain.

She was glad he had not insisted on the removal of her chemise last night for even in that darkened room he would have seen and known. Her shame. She glanced away, knowing the black anger of it would be showing in her eyes and she did not wish for him to see.

The mark on his jaw shone opaque against the firelight, lost slightly in the growth of stubble. If he grew a beard, it would be gone entirely. She was glad he had not. Had he wanted to he could have erased all memory of her for ever. As it was he must look every day into his reflection and be reminded.

The futility of everything blended with the brandy, a melancholy covering all she had hoped for once. He was as beautiful as he had been then, in every way, strong and self-assured, although the mantle of aristocracy gave him an added allure.

Shallow, she knew, but it was a fact. With a man like this she could be safe.

Sense reined in fantasy. He was all but promised to the beautiful and clever Lady Acacia Bellowes-Browne, a woman who would suit him exactly and in every way. She wondered if he ever thought of the hurried marriage in the village by the river where Mademoiselle Sandrine Mercier had married Monsieur Nathanael Colbert, two names plucked from a half-truth and settled in the register like impostors.

At this very moment all he looked was angry.

'Every time you come into my life, Sandrine, it seems chaos follows.'

'I am no longer Sandrine.'

'Are you not?' He came closer, the largeness of him disconcerting. England seemed full of small men with the smell of a woman about them, the indolence of life written upon their skin in softness, the bloom of ease apparent. Nathaniel Lindsay had none of these qualities. He could have been transported here from an earlier time, the menace and threat of him magnified in a room filled with books and quiet pursuits. She would be most unwise to ever think that a lord like this could offer safety after all that she had done to him.

'What other woman of the *ton* would dress as a lad and walk the back streets of hopelessness in the midnight hours? Your father must be demented to allow it.'

At that she laughed. 'The days of a man's ordinance over me are long gone, Lord Lindsay.'

'Even a husband's?'

She had wondered when he would mention it, had been expecting him to from the very outset, but the word still made her blanch, the beat of her heart hurrying with the reference.

'If our marriage was deemed to be a binding agreement, then our years apart must allow grounds for question. But given the circumstances, I should imagine it was not.'

He smiled, but the steel in his eyes hardened.

'Why were you there, at the brothel?' She needed to know if he was friend or foe.

'Two women were killed a month ago beside the Thames in Whitechapel. I was following up a lead to find the man who did it.'

Every word he said made their relationship more dangerous. 'Do you have names?'

'No.'

'Other clues, then?'

'I am looking for a tall and well-heeled man. His hair is dark.'

'Such a one has been seen by the children we have rescued on a number of occasions.' She wondered why she told him.

'Which is why you were at the de Clare ball, no doubt. Scouting?'

'You read my intentions with too much ease for comfort of mind, Lord Lindsay.'

'Do I, Miss Northrup?' Something had changed between them in just this single second. She felt the tension in the room shift to something less certain.

'What happened after I last saw you with Guy Lebansart?'

'I grew up. I paid the debts I owed and I grew up.'

'You sacrificed others to save me? Why?' Anger creased his brow.

She felt the breath in her hollow, felt the beat of her heart flatten into some new and risky unease, and did not speak.

'I never asked that of you.' Said in the man-

ner of a man who was not comfortable with in-
debtedness. 'Nor did I want it from you.'

She had had enough. 'You think that you
might control everything, my lord? You think
that people should only march to your drum,
the drum of the morally justified? Are you
now one of those men who cannot see another
side of an argument, the side where good and
bad mix in together to create a new word, an
in-between word, that allows life?' Whirling
around, she went to stand at the window. Part
of her thought to slip through it into safety, but
another part understood that without explanation she might never be free of him and he was
dangerous. To the life she had built which depended to a large extent on her being accepted
by those she mingled with.

'After leaving you I stayed in Perpignan. I
was shocked by all that happened, you understand. Celeste's family needed time to know
of the demise of their loved one and I needed
a space to myself before…' She stopped.

'Before you returned to England?'

Jamie. Jamie. Jamie.

Under each and every word said his small
and beloved face lingered and it was all she
could do to hold him safe.

'I have forged a life here. My life. Once, a very long time ago, I was someone else.'

A traitor. A wife. A victim.

A woman who had used every part of her wiles to save the father of her baby. She did not flinch as he watched her. She did not think of the marks on her breast or the weeks of fever that had followed. She thought only of Jamie.

As if Nathaniel Lindsay's fingers had a mind of their own they went to his chin and traced the damage. 'I thought that I knew you then, but now…'

'Now we are strangers travelling in different directions, my lord.'

Away from each other? Away to safety.

Turn and go now. Turn and go before he touches you and before the quiet way he gives his words makes you foolish. It is the only way that Jamie can stay safe.

With a quick snatch at the curtain, she lifted her leg across the sill and was gone.

Nat stood and watched her run, her shadow barely there against the line of trees, blending in the moonlight.

Even with Acacia he had never felt this connection, this need to protect her from all and sundry. Cassandra Northrup made him crazy, witless and sad, yet the feel of her slight body against his in the warm waters of the high pool above Bagnères-de-Bigorre lingered.

Shimmering against reason.

They had gone there by chance, a traveller's tale remembered, a small, ancient and lonely pool set amongst the mountain scrub, steam rising like God's breath from the very bowels of a restless earth.

She had forged on ahead from the little house by the river, trying to escape him, he was to understand with time, hurrying along the mountain passes without looking back, though when he had found her a good two hours later she had given no explanation and he had not wanted to ask for one.

After that they had moved with their own thoughts across the landscape, always climbing higher. An image of Alph the sacred river running to measureless caverns and sunless seas took his imagination. Sandrine was like a sylph, light of foot and pure of heart, her hair in the grey mists the only bright and shining beacon.

His wife.

He had never been married before and the

troth was surprising in its power. She was young, he knew that, but under her youth there was wisdom and discernment born from an adversity he could only wonder at.

His.

For better or for worse.

He quickened his pace. Already she was thirty feet in front of him and the slope was steepening, but to his left was the grotto he had found many years before, the steam even from this distance visible.

'There.' He pointed, and she shaded her eyes and looked, a smile rewarding his discovery.

'We can take a bath?'

He nodded and took her hand because the shale was treacherous and he did not wish for her to slip.

Later, in the cold winters of London, he would think of this time and try to remember each and every moment of it. Back then the relief of another chance at life after their sickness had made him feel exhilarated.

He could smell the sulphur as they came across the last rise, the warmth of air in the wind blowing towards them. Like an invitation, and just for a moment, he imagined them as the only people upon the entire planet, lost in the universe. He wondered if the fevers had taken his reason because he seldom thought like this, the flowery rhetoric of the Romantic poets on his tongue. Perhaps it was Sandrine who made him such but he didn't like to think of what that might mean.

Nat's side ached, and he still felt hot, but a day out amongst the clouds had revitalised and settled him.

'Will others come?' Her voice was small.

'Not now.' Already the light was falling. Another hour and it would be gone completely.

When she smiled, he smiled back, his aching bones crying out for a warm soak in a mineral pool. She dipped in her fingers, the ruined hand swallowed by opaque water, nestled in heat.

'You have been here before?'

'A long while ago.'

'Is your home near?'

This time he merely shook his head and sat down, taking off his boots and placing his socks carefully within the leather so that they did not get damp.

She was watching him, her eyes filled with delight. A joyous Sandrine was so different from the one he more usually saw, the dimples in her cheeks deep and the quiet creases of laughter charming.

'Put your clothes under mine when you have them off. That way they will stay dry.'

Within a moment he was naked, wading into the water and dipping down. She had turned away, allowing for privacy, but he did not care. Closing his eyes, he waited till she joined him.

'I cannot ever remember feeling so good.' Her words were quiet as she lay back, spreading her hair across the surface, like a mermaid or an enchantress, the colour in each strand darkened by the water. She had not pushed off from the bottom for every other part of her body save her face and neck was hidden from him.

Most women of his acquaintance would have simpered and hesitated, a lack of clothes precluding all enjoyment. But not her. She simply took what was offered with a brave determination, the mist beading her eyelashes and small drops settling on her cheeks and lips.

'It is said in these parts that this pool contains the soul of a sea sprite who lost her lover.' Another flight of ridiculous fancy. He grimaced.

'How?'

'The sprite changed him into a merman so that they might always be together, but his jealous wife threw flames upon his form and he dissolved into steam.'

'Water and steam. They still live together?'

Sandrine's hand came up from the pool and she cradled both elements. 'Legends and science. My mother would have peered into this pool to see what lived inside of each drop.'

'The new and unseen frontier of science?'

'You know of this? She looked puzzled and faintly incredulous.

'When I am not killing people I can be found reading.'

Her laughter rang across the quiet, echoing back. 'A warrior and a scholar. If you were to go to the salons of the wealthy, Nathanael Colbert, you would be besieged by women. Celeste would have been one of those had she lived.'

'How did your cousin die?'

'By her own hand. Baudoin's brother Louis was her first lover and when he was killed she had no more heart for life.'

'Difficult for you. The one left.'

She did not answer, but in her eyes there was such grief that he moved closer and took her hand, waiting till she regained composure. All the things that she did not say were written in hard anger upon her face.

'How did this happen?' His thumb traced the line of her ruined finger because he knew that to speak of such travesty would be a balm.

'Baudoin and his brother were always at odds with one another over my cousin. Once, when we first came to Nay, I tried to drag Celeste back from getting involved in an argument and Anton slashed out at me.'

Anguish solidified inside of him, and he attempted for her sake to push it down. 'I see you holding it now and then, rubbing at the finger that is missing?'

She smiled. 'It hurts sometimes, a phantom pain as if it is still there.'

The small fragility of her hand made the wound seem even more mindless. The ring of his mother's that she wore was far too big and he touched it.

'I will have it resized, Sandrine. So you do not lose it.'

Puzzlement in her eyes was tinged with surprise. 'I should not expect you to honour a marriage that was forced upon you when you were too sick to resist.'

'The church may disagree.'

Their world stood still, steam the only thing moving between them, up into the growing blackness. Their shared night-time kiss also shimmered in the promise.

'A poor reward, no doubt, for all your endeavours to save me.' The grasp of her fingers slid about his own.

'Ah, but it could have been worse. You might have been old or ugly or had the tongue of a shrew.'

She laughed.

'No. I think on balance I was not at all hard done by.'

The lustrous colour of her hair caught at them, claiming him, binding them as one.

Alive.

She was still alive and so was he and she was pleased her attempt to escape him had come to nothing. In the silence above the world she allowed her head to rest upon his chest, listening to his heart.

The beat of vitality against her ear, the course of blood and hope and energy. It had been so long since she had been held this way, with care, like a porcelain doll shimmering in the wind. With only a small nudge she might shatter apart completely and she did not want to move. No, here she wanted to know what it felt like to breathe in the sensual and be rewarded by its promise. The lump in her throat thickened. She did not love Nathanael Colbert and he did not love her back but they were man and wife, a pair beneath the gentle hand of God, and in this, His place, a natural pool of light and water and warmth.

For so long she had been fighting alone. For all the months of Nay and then the year before that, her mother's death embedded in her sadness.

Could she not let it go for one moment on a hillside in the wilds of the Pyrenees and in the company of a man who looked at her as if she was truly beautiful?

No ties save that of a marriage that would never be real. If she survived this flight to Perpignan she would return to England, ruined by all the accounts that would follow her, she was sure of it. But would she ever again be offered the chance of this?

The skin across his arms was brown and hard, the indigo of his tattoo strangely distorted in the water. She touched it now, traced the curl of serpent with one finger and then leant her mouth to the task.

Tasting him.

He breathed in deeply, and Cassandra felt the power of which Celeste had spoken all those months before. Not a limited sovereignty or a slight one. When her fingers slipped higher to his face she outlined the features: his nose, his cheeks, the swell of his lips and the long line of his throat.

His eyes watched her, fathomless, twin mirrors of the sky and the water and the mist, but fire lurked there, too, and it was building.

'I am only a man, Sandrine. So take care that you do not cross boundaries you have no wish for me to traverse.'

'What if I do?'

There, it was said and she would not take it back, not even when the flicker of wariness crossed into grey and she saw in his soul the first thought of 'why?'.

If he asks, I shall walk straight out of this pool.

But he remained quiet and the turn of hardness, his sex, budded beneath the limed water.

It was what she needed, this truth of reaction, no whispered lies between them stating a future that could never be. For this moment she felt like a woman reborn, the girl in her pushed back by a feeling that was new, creeping into the place between her legs and into her stomach. Heavy. Languid. Damp.

Lost in the transfer of all she had suffered.

And in control of everything.

He did not speak because he was a man who understood small nuances. It was his job after all, seeking truth and finding exactly what it was those buried under the shifting tides of war needed to survive.

Sandrine needed oblivion, and he needed her to find it. It was simple. A translation of grief.

She was weightless against him, her thinness in the water disguised. He was glad he could only feel: the small mounds of her breasts, the flat plane of her stomach, her long legs draped around his waist as if they had a mind all of their own.

Opened to him. Waiting.

He wrapped the fine length of her hair about his wrist, tethering her, gentling her, the cold in the air and the heat of their bodies making light work of the joining, and when his lips came down upon her upturned mouth he did not hold back.

He was in her, tasting, her throat arched upwards and their breath mingled. He knew the moment he had her assent, for she began to shiver. In her ardency her fingers scraped down the side of his arms.

'I want to know what it is like to have a husband.' The honesty in her words undid him.

No pretentiousness, the grandiose and flowery allowances of various ladies he had known pushed aside by a simple truth. She did not play games or set rules or say one thing, but mean another. Danger and hardship had done away with all the extraneous.

Hot. He felt hot from the pool and her skin and the building need inside him. 'I would not wish to hurt you.'

She smiled at that, the dimples in her cheeks deep, and steam across the coldness of night lifting around them. 'I know that you won't. It is why I want it to be you.'

With care, his fingers dipped, the softness of woman and the heat there, and she tensed, her eyes sharpening as though pain might follow and when it didn't she urged him further, a small sigh of release and surprise.

She was tight and tense, her eyes a clear and startled turquoise as she watched him, measuring, challenging, her hips lifting to allow him in farther though her brow furrowed as he found the hard nub of her desire.

She stilled him.

'What is this?'

'You, Sandrine, the centre of you.'

Relaxing even as he spoke, she allowed him closer, the feel of her body against his, her breasts more generous than he had thought them.

'Beautiful.'

Exchanging his hand for his manhood, he pushed wide, edging inwards, filling the space of her. When her arms pulled him in he knew that he had her and, twisting his body, he came in deeper.

With the water and the bubbles and the steam about them, both lost their tapering hold on reason, the final absolution as she went to pieces, beaching waves of rigid need, and then was quiet.

He held her motionless as he took his own relief, his face held upward so that the fine mist of night cooled him, his groan of pleasure involuntary.

'God, help us.' He had never felt like this before with anyone, never wanted to start again and have her impaled upon him, for all the hours of the night and the dawn, only his.

He should have withdrawn, should have given his seed to the water where it would wither and die in the heat. And instead…

If she were fertile then a part of him would grow.

But she did not let him think. 'Take me again on the bank in the cold.' Her voice was soft and her tongue licked at the space about his chin.

A thin, brave and pale siren with no idea at all as to how much she had affected him. Lifting her into his arms, he came from the pool in a cloud of steam and laid her down in the nearly night and gazed.

'You are so very lovely.' He whispered the words, honesty in every syllable, and when she smiled he found the hidden folds between her legs and tasted her. Sandrine. Salty and sweet and young.

Much later he dressed her, carefully so that the cold did not creep into softness. He had marked her as his, the red whorls of his loving standing out on the paleness of her skin, telling the story of long and passionate hours. But already the dawn birds called across the wide mountain valleys, signalling in the light.

'I did not know it could be like that.' Her voice was guarded. 'After Nay I was not a virgin.'

The rawness of her confession grated against the new day. A confidence she did not wish to share, but had felt the need to? He frowned.

'No one could live in that hovel and remain...untouched, though Celeste soon worked out a way to protect me from them.'

'How?'

'She began a relationship with Louis Baudoin and insisted I sleep in a small room off their own.' Taking in a deep breath she continued on. 'I think she thought the accident in the carriage was her fault somehow. She had wanted to take a detour off the main road and it was there that the horses stumbled down the hill. Her father and his godson were killed and Louis Baudoin found us just before it snowed.'

'A saviour?' He hoped she would not hear the irony.

'He took us home, and Celeste was grateful.'

'And you?'

'I was grateful to her.'

When people lied they often glanced down before they did so. Their body language changed, too, the arm crossing the chest in an effort at defence. Nathaniel saw all of this in Sandrine, and when she did not answer he did not press her, but the joy of communion wilted a little in the deception and in her confessions.

With the wind behind her and the shadow of her hair across her cheeks she suddenly did not look as young as she always had before. But she was not quite finished.

'My cousin was of an age when the adventures of life are sometimes sacrificed to the safer and more conventional. I could not save her.'

Nat stood and took her hand, holding it firmly as she tried to loosen the grip.

'It is over now, Sandrine, and the past is behind us.'

But she only shook her head. 'No, Nathanael, it is here right at our heels, and if you had any sense at all you would leave immediately and escape me.'

His laughter echoed about the lonely and barren hills.

Chapter Five

Maureen confronted her the morning after she had gone to the St Auburn town house, deep marks of worry across her brow and dark eyes fixed upon her lips.

'You were so late home last night. I can hardly recognise who you have become, Cassie, and I do not think you know it yourself, either.'

Her rebuke stung. 'This is not an easy task, Reena. There are so many who need—'

'To be saved?' A question. 'And what will be your salvation when you are caught in the lad's clothes far from home and I cannot find you?'

High emotion changed a careful diction so that the words slurred together unfinished and disjointed. Realising this, Maureen reined her anger in, the hands she used so much in communication hard up against her ears, pressing, and the guilt that had been Cassandra's constant companion since the accident bloomed.

'I cannot properly hear what people say any more, Cassie. Mama was certain that I would grow out of my affliction, but it is worsening.'

'If Mama was still here she would know what to do, but she isn't. She's gone,' Cassandra shouted back, for after an evening sparring with Nathaniel Lindsay she was heedless. 'It was all my fault that she died. I was the one who did that.'

They had seldom spoken of the day of the accident, the memory too painful for them both. Their beautiful and clever mama falling down upon the floor, her eyes wide open with surprise and pain and then nothing. Save Reena with her hands on her ears in exactly the same way she held them now, her face creased with disbelief.

The laughter was unexpected.

'Mama's science is what killed her, Cassie. Mama and her foolish insistence on having us help her.'

The shock of the words kept Cassandra still.

'Alysa only thought about her experiments.

Don't you remember that? She lived in her laboratory. Her scientific discoveries were her babies so much more than we ever could be and the thought of saving the world soul by soul through uncovering unseen sicknesses was what drove her. If she had not been killed in that particular accident, then there would have been another.'

Such revelations amazed Cassie. 'You never told me this.'

'I tried to because I could see that you thought it was your fault, but you loved her too much to listen and then you got sick.'

Heartsick. Body-sick. Soul-sick.

Leached of life by guilt and then by shame.

'I should be rejoicing in my affliction in any case and not decrying it. I would have never met Kenyon otherwise for I would have heard his horse behind me and got off the path. What a loss that would have been.'

The day just kept getting stranger.

'Kenyon Riley?'

'Of course. I am getting older, old enough to imagine I should never have the chance of a family. I love him and he has asked me to marry him.'

Pieces of a puzzle clicked into place. Kenyon's presence at the school, his interest in everything that they did, his generosity and his kindness.

'You have been distracted lately, Cassie. I wanted to tell you, but you were never here. You were always dressed in your boy's clothes and out in the night, helping others.'

Mama. Maureen. Kenyon.

My God, she had missed all the signs of change.

'There is a problem, however, and I think it is only fair that you hear of it from me. There are whispers in places that say you were the woman in Lord Lindsay's bed in that whorehouse in Whitechapel, and they are gaining in traction. Kenyon has tried to douse the rumour, but it seems you were seen.'

Maureen's careful diction made the accusations sound so much worse, each rounded word ringing out the ruin.

'Tell me it is not true, Cassie, and we can refute it together. I can say you were here with me and that they were mistaken...' Her voice petered off as Cassandra shook her head and anger lit her dark eyes.

'He forced you?'

'No.'

'You wanted him?'

'No.'

'Then why?'

Because I was abused once by monsters who held no mind for a young, thin, sick and frightened girl. Because Nathanael Colbert saved me from hell and we were married under other names in a town I can barely remember. Because I betrayed others to save his life. Because I have killed men by my hand and by my words and he hates me for it all.

That is what she could have said, might have even tried to had her brother not have chosen that very second to interrupt them and come tumbling into the room with a parrot upon his shoulder.

'I was given this by a sailor in the park who had come from India and wanted to go back again without the bother of a bird. Sixpence, he charged me, and he said I was to call him "Mine".'

At the sound of his name the bird lunged from his perch on Rodney's arm up on to the gold clip in Maureen's hair, pecking at the glitter to create havoc. And Cassie knew without a single doubt that any moment of truth was well and truly lost.

'Mine. Mine. Mine', she heard them both calling as she slipped through the doorway and left.

Cassandra lay in bed that night and thought of all that Maureen had said. If the gossip about her were to become widespread, what would happen? Nathaniel Lindsay would hardly be stepping forward with an offer of his hand. Again.

Wonderful and terrible.

The day had been that. Maureen's good news balanced against her bad. The guilt felt about her mother's death lost into the wonder of Reena meeting Kenyon Riley and all because she did not hear the hoofbeats of his horse as they came from behind her. Despite everything else, Cassie smiled and rubbed at the china shard Nathanael had threaded for her in the tiny village of Saint Estelle.

They had come down into the settlement late in the afternoon, the thin sunlight slanting on to their faces as they walked in silence after their night at the pools. Cassandra had not dared to break with words the magic that danced about every part of her body.

This was what she had heard of in the ballads and in the books. This crawling, sensuous, languid warmth that sifted through everything and left her different.

She wished they might find a room somewhere, alone, and begin all over again. The punching throb of need made her groan, and he turned.

'Are you hurt?'

The redness began at her breast and crept up on to her cheeks, a wave of heat similar to that she had felt last night. Unstoppable. She was like a woman in a story book, a woman with little will of her own and a singular wish for the feelings expressed in the works of the Romantic poets Celeste and she had read under the candlelight.

Thrilling.

Please.

The word coiled inside her like a snake waiting to strike.

Please. Please. Please.

She saw the moment he understood what it was she hid, blue darkening across silver in a will all of its own.

Lust it might be for him, but for her love held on at the edges, grasping tentatively. The feel of the ring against her skin deepened it, a circle that held them together, caught in the company of each other, pledged to God.

And by flesh now, the feel of him within her, the building joy of need, the hours of play and delight so different from anything she had known at Nay.

She shook away the darkness. No. She would not think of that again.

'I will find us a room.' His voice sounded strained and unnatural.

This time the feeling was different. This time they circled each other fully dressed in a chamber that was…comfortable. Now instead of a strange world far from the one they knew, a certain familiarity crept in. The crystal of the glasses. The bed with its feather quilts. A window where the blinds had been drawn across the remains of the day; curtains of floral damask much like the ones hanging in the library room at home. Bread and wine sat upon a gilded tray on the table.

The consequences of choices already made settled in. One day she would be back in London and this would all be a memory.

She began to unbutton her shirt, but he stopped her.

'We will eat first.'

First.

She shook her head. She was not hungry for food or wine. She did not want to wait until they had supped and spoken, all the normal things that happened in a relationship. This was not normal, the aching lust that coursed through her and made her want to lunge at him and take everything that his body could offer hers. She wanted him inside, moving; she wanted to feel all those things she had last night and this morning when her mind for once had flown away from thought and into a place that was only feeling.

No past or future, only now.

'We have time to—'

She stopped him. With her fingers across his lips. Pressed hard.

'No.' Her other hand unbuttoned his shirt and came inside, the warmth beguiling. Yesterday he had flicked her nipples with his forefinger and she had liked it. Today she did the same to him, measuring his heartbeat as it quickened.

'Tonight is by my bidding.'

The slate-grey darkened, the last light from a dying sun slanting through a gap in the curtains and reaching the skin on his chest where she had peeled away clothing.

'Like the daughters of Achelous?'

'The sirens?' She laughed. 'Dangerous and beautiful?' He knew the old legends of Greece and the names of the gods. For a second she wondered just exactly who he was, this man dressed in clothes that had seen better days, but when she kneeled to undo his trousers she forgot about such intrigue entirely.

He was her husband and he was ready for her, sprung hard against lust, nothing hidden. A gift offered without payment or coercion. Or hurt. Legal. Sanctioned. Authorised.

She laid her fingers around his shaft and brought it to her tongue, licking the ridges and the smoothness, finding the essence; and when he swore roundly she brought him in deeper.

Hell, Nathaniel thought, his world spinning in a way it never had before, the sweet feel of yearning drumming in his ears. Wild curls hid Sandrine from him, trails in gold and red, her slender shoulders bent in concentration to all that she gave. He knew she wanted control, but in another moment his restraint would break and he had to give her back more than just his own relief.

Guiding her face away from swollen flesh, he lifted her chin and she stood. He had no clothes on and she was fully dressed, small webs of repaired fabric standing out against the light. Placing his mouth across hers, he slanted the kiss, his fingers running across the fine lines of her throat and bringing her closer.

'Love me, Sandrine.' Whispered. Gentle. Allowing more than simple lust.

'I do.'

She was so light as he lifted her, a shadow of a woman, but tall with it. He brought her to the bed and sat her down, and when her hands went to the buttons at her shirt he stopped her.

'My turn.'

She did not argue.

Five buttons and one missing. Beneath the cotton was sheer lawn and lace, repaired like the rest of her clothes, but of a quality that told him of a life led before. The pad of his finger lingered on the stitching, complex, intricate, the sort of thing his mother might have worn had she lived.

The straps were thin and of satin and he slid them across her shoulders so that the chemise drooped and her breasts were there, peaked and perfect. He cupped his hand around one feeling its form, admiring the curve of skin and the unexpected smattering of freckles.

The tip-tilt of her nose as she looked at him made him smile. A girl who was the most beautiful woman in the world. The narrowness of her waist, the slender length of her arms, the elegance of neck.

This was Sandrine.

A goddess lost into the wilderness and now refound.

He traced his initials into the cream of her skin, *NL*, and she looked up in puzzlement.

'Once I was someone else,' he explained.

'And I was, too,' she responded, the rightness of their coupling underwritten by truth. 'But now all I want to be is loved well.'

He lifted her onto his knees, slipping off her trousers and socks and boots so that she sat naked and waiting. He liked how she did not hold her legs together tightly or stiffen as his fingers came between them, exploring.

'Is this well enough?' he asked as he found the core of her in the hard nub of need. 'Is this what you want?' he added as he began to move faster and faster, the rhythm changing just as he thought she was about to come apart.

Wet for him and swollen. He could feel the throb inside and the heat.

And when she nodded he simply placed her upon his cock and drove in, the finesse transformed to something much stronger and more basic. It was not knowledge that brought them together now, but an ancient magic with no rational thought, and he cried out as her body clenched about his, taking all that he offered and more.

He took her again in the night and once in the morning when the first rays of sunshine woke them. He had not slept with a woman for so many hours in his life, his more normal caution and vigilance taking him from a bed well before they asked for more than he might want to give. But with Sandrine they spooned together in the cold and lonely hours and when they awoke their bodies called, the quick burst of need and the slow sating after relief.

Once on waking he found her looking at him, as though she wanted to remember every piece of who he was.

'Stay with me for ever.' The words were out

before he knew them to be and she placed his hand upon her heart in answer.

'Here. You will always be here.'

'Do you promise?'

Nodding, she simply rolled over on top of him and all that had been magical before began again.

Cassandra awoke with tears running down her cheeks and the cold London morning bearing down. No longer in France. No longer in the place of dreams and promises, the steam bath above Bagnères-de-Bigorre and the curtained room in Saint Estelle.

Avalon. The vaulted ceilings and the shining marbled Gothic arches.

A noise made her turn, and James was at her doorway, a teddy bear held in one hand so that his furry legs dragged along the floor.

'Mummy.'

'I am here, darling.' She pulled back the sheet and waited until he came inside, tucking the warmth about him when he was settled. His small roundness pressed into her, the smell of slumber upon him.

'I dreamed we were in France.' His pale

grey eyes watched her, dark hair standing on end from sleep.

'Once we were, my love. Once it was just you and I there and I knew from the very second I saw you that I should love you for ever.'

He giggled. 'You always say that.'

'And I always mean it.'

'Nigel said his daddy still lives in France. But I said mine was dead.'

The worm of dread turned. 'Well, you have so many others who love you, sweetheart. Mummy. Maureen. Anne. Granddad. Rodney. The cook. Nigel's mummy.'

'But a daddy is special. Nigel said that they were.'

Lord Nathaniel Lindsay. More than special. She would have to tell him, she knew that she would, but not yet. Not while Jamie was still hers to love and hold like this, the secrets of the past hidden in a corner where they were unable to escape and ruin everything.

And if Nathaniel took their son away...?

She shook her head and, drawing her fingers up into the shape of a spider, began to recite a children's ditty, liking the laughter that followed.

Chapter Six

'Chris Hanley said what?'

Nat tried to curb the panic in his voice as Stephen answered.

'He said that he saw Cassandra Northrup creeping from the Brown Street boarding house as though the very devil was on her tail the night of the murder.'

'What the hell was Hanley doing there?'

Hawk began to laugh. 'He was out on the town with a group of friends, but your question precludes other more pressing ones, Nat. If, for example, your lady was not present you might have asked if he was crazy to be so mistaken? As a judge, I would infer from your words that the accusation was true.'

'Cassandra Northrup is hardly my lady.'

His mind whirled as Stephen continued to

speak. 'The ruination of her reputation might only be a minor concern when stacked up against such a killing.'

'Do people believe Hanley?'

'I'd like to say no, but I think that they are beginning to. Reginald Northrup has made no attempt at silencing his friend either, which is telling. I took it on myself to find out a little of the Northrups and if Reginald himself stands to gain anything from any discrediting of the brother's family. One daughter is almost deaf, the second one is married and living in Scotland and the son is still a minor. Cassandra Northrup's ruination is irrelevant for I am certain Cowper would have made a will stating his preferred guardians for Rodney and for the trustees of his estate.'

'Is it the title he wants? From all accounts the Northrups are not as rich as he is.'

'No, not that. Just the influence, I am presuming, for the title is more than safe. Rodney is the direct heir, but there is another more pressing fact that you should know, Nathaniel, given your recent championing of the youngest Northrup daughter. Cassandra Northrup may not be the lady that you think she is. She is reputed to take many more risks than she should.'

'Risks?'

'She does not seem to give much account to her reputation. It seems she is not averse to wandering the same streets the prostitutes do in order to save some of them. Kenyon Riley was touchy when I asked him further about it.'

'You saw Riley?'

'Yesterday at White's. He bought rounds for all and sundry and I had the feeling some personal celebration was in the air. He spends a lot of time with the Northrups so perhaps he has finally decided to offer for one of the daughters.'

The wheel turned further and further. Cassandra Northrup had become the beauty Nat had predicted she would all those years before and even encumbered with two failed marriages she was...unmatched.

Swearing, he poured himself another drink.

She ransacked him with her beauty. That was the trouble. The history between them had also had a hand, their marriage, their trysts around Saint Estelle and the small villages before Perpignan, hours when he had imagined her as his forever wife safe at St Auburn and providing timely heirs for a title steeped in the tradition of first-born boys.

Lord, what groundless hopes. In every meeting thus far she had never given him an inkling that she hankered for more between them other than the safe keeping of hidden secrets arising from betrayal.

And now a further problem. She was innocent of the murder of the man at the brothel, but could he just leave her to fight the accusations herself? He knew that he could not.

'Is our membership in the Venus Club complete, Stephen?

'Yes?'

'When do they meet again?'

'This Saturday. I thought to go there after making a showing at the Forsythe ball.'

'I will accompany you then. I would like a chat with Christopher Hanley.'

'So you will still be involving yourself with Cassandra Northrup's plight?' The laughter in his friend's eyes made Nat wary. Sometimes Stephen had a knack of finding out things from him that he did not wish to divulge.

'There may be no one else to help her.'

Hawk raised his glass. 'Then I drink to an outcome that will be of benefit to you both.'

Nathaniel wondered what Stephen might have made of the fact that they had once been married and that high up on the foothills of the Pyrenees their troths had been consummated with more than just a nominal effort. He wished he might speak of it now, but there would be no point in the confidence. Sandrine had chosen her pathway and it had wound well away from his. Still, he would not want to see her made victim for a crime she had not committed.

He swallowed, for his logic made no sense. She had betrayed England and then carried on with her life with hardly a backward glance. He should not trust her.

A ring of the doorbell brought his butler into the library.

'There is a Miss Maureen Northrup here to see you, my lord. She will not come through, however, but would like a quick word in the foyer.'

Standing, Nat looked at Hawk, who lifted his glass with a smile. 'A further complication?'

Outside, the same dark-eyed girl at Albi's ball stood, her maid at her side and her hands wringing at the fabric in her skirt. Underneath a wide hat he could see her face and she looked neither happy not rested.

'Miss Northrup.'

'Thank you for seeing me, Lord Lindsay. I will be as brief as I can be. Is there a room where we might have a moment's privacy?'

'There is.' He opened the door to his left and shepherded her into the blue salon, wondering at all the conventions being broken for an unmarried woman to be alone here. He did not shut the door.

'I wish to know what your intentions are regarding my sister, my lord?' She did not tarry with the mundane.

'I have none.'

He thought she swallowed, and she paled further at his reply.

'Then I want you to stay well away from Cassandra, sir. She does not need your dubious threats.'

'Threats? She told you I had been threatening her?'

'Not in as many words. But unless you have some hold upon her I cannot see why she would have been willingly in your bed in that house of disrepute off the Whitechapel Road for any other reason.'

This Northrup daughter was as brave as her sister, her eyes directly on his face and no blush at all upon her cheeks.

Her voice was strange, he thought, the diction so precise. Then he saw her glance upon his lips and he remembered. She was deaf. Deaf and brave, he corrected, and trying with all her might to protect her family.

'I was helping her. A man had been murdered in the room opposite and San...Cassandra would have been implicated had she been found there. I bundled her into my bed and pretended...'

He could not go on. This was the strangest conversation he had ever had with anyone before.

'Pretended...? You said "pretended"?' She mulled the word over, the light coming on in her dark eyes as she did so. 'I see, my lord. I had thought...' Again she stopped. 'Thank you for your time, Lord Lindsay. I do appreciate it.'

With that she simply glided out through the door, gesturing to her wide-eyed maid to follow and was gone, the clock in the hall ringing out the hour of one in the afternoon. The butler looked as puzzled as he did.

'If Miss Northrup returns, do you wish to know of it, sir?'

'I doubt she will be back, Haines, but if she comes send her through to me.'

Stephen still sat where Nat had left him and from the look on his face he had heard the whole thing.

'If Cassandra Northrup was with you, Nat, I should imagine your intentions are nothing like those you regaled the oldest Miss Northrup with? You have not taken a woman to bed in years.'

A reprimand. Given with the very best of intentions. He could no longer lie to Hawk.

'Once, Cassandra Northrup and I were married. In France.'

By the look in his friend's eyes this was the last confession that he had been expecting. 'Are you still?'

'It was never annulled.'

'I see.'

The silence in the room heightened, a heavy blanket of question.

'She had been captured by a group of bandits in the Languedoc region and dealt with badly. I was trying to protect her.'

'Something that you are still doing here.'

'Perhaps.'

'Then take care, Nathaniel, for society can be most intolerant to a woman who would live outside its rules. Even one who is both beautiful and clever.'

Saint Estelle had been small and run-down, a mountain town of old buildings and kind people.

In the morning after they had eaten they had walked along the river and he had found a shard of blue-green pottery at the water's edge.

'If I could buy you a tourmaline, Sandrine, I would, because that gemstone is the exactly the shade of your eyes. But as I am penniless, this will have to do.'

She took it carefully, with the hand that was not ruined, and held it up to look at. 'Gemstone pottery?' Her laughter hung in the earliness of the day and warmed his heart. 'A priceless gift that I will keep for ever.'

'For ever is a long time.' Sadness had settled in the corners of his mind. He wanted to hold her away from danger and keep her safe. He wanted to take her to St Auburn and make her understand exactly whom she had married, the coffers of the place filled with the treasure of the past in an unending array of wealth, diamonds, gold and silver and every gemstone in between. He wondered what she would make of the expectations inherent in his title and conversely what those at the castle might make of her. Especially his grandfather.

'Tonight I will find some leather and fashion a hole through the top so that you can wear it as a pendant.'

Her hair had caught the wind and the many-coloured lights of it tumbled wild with her curls, the length reaching the contour of her hips.

'Mama always insisted that one gift required another in return. She said that in the giving of a present there should also be the taking of happiness.'

He stood still as her hand came against his cheek, tracing the line of his throat downwards.

'The gift of the power of womanhood is one I could bestow upon you if you should so desire it, Nathanael.' Beneath the laughter in her words there was another cadence, full of promise. 'My cousin Celeste used to say that I should find it one day, this knowledge of the

sensual, and that men would not be able to refuse such an authority from me.'

'She was right.' Gravity had crept in under
humour and he could hear the steady beat of
his own heart in his ears.

'So you accept?'

'I do.'

They were far from the village and he had
seen no sign of others for many miles. Besides,
the road out of Saint Estelle lay upon the opposite bank of the river, past the line of trees,
out of sight.

Last night had been frenzied and passionate
and furious. Today a languid peace reigned, a
quiet acceptance of each other's needs.

'Come.' She held out her hand and he took
it, following her into the shadow of the trees
until they reached an overhang of cliff, the
rocky outcrop of the Pyrenees sheltering a little bowl of meadow. It was noticeably warmer.

'Here, away from the wind we can love each
other.' Bringing two blankets from her bag, she
laid them down as a bed.

Within a moment she had removed her
clothes, lying on the wool without any sense
of shame, burnished like an angel from one

of the old religious paintings that graced his grandfather's library.

Reaching for his fingers, she placed them upon her right breast and leaned into the touch. His other hand she splayed in the warmth of the space between her legs, her thighs apart and waiting. 'I am yours for the day, *monsieur*. I am yours until the sun lies upon the horizon and the dusk is reached. My gift for your gift.'

Positioning the other blanket to keep out the cold, his fingers began to move with a will of their own, up into the warmth of her, up into the swollen wet darkness where feminine magic lingered. She did not draw back. He slipped in farther and heard her sharp intake of breath. Playing her tenderly and feeling the answer of her muscles against his hand, the first tremble of release as frenzy tightened. Taking ownership. He did not let her move away as her whole body shuddered into climax, roiling waves clenching skin to muscle.

She cried out, once and then again, her head arched back so that daylight filled her, the sweat of climax dampening her skin and making her rigid with lust.

The scent of her between them, the hard erectness of nipples, the loss of self into a frenzy of feeling. Shivering need brought her arms about him, her nails gouging trails into his shoulder. Joined. For ever. Locked into union.

Moments passed in silence, the heat of her slackening to limpness.

When he brought his mouth onto the peak of her right breast, she simply clasped her hands about his head and nudged him closer. Like she might do a suckling baby, guided to the source.

Quiet. Still. Primal. The reclamation of all that had been once before and now was again. The gift of belonging. The heavy punch of sex and now the softer pull of place. Home. With Sandrine. He shut his eyes and took the offered gift, grateful and indebted.

In all of his life he had never felt as loved.

They woke to the sound of evening bird-song, the dusk across their blankets. With slow care she moved atop his manhood, filling herself with the largeness, moving in her own rhythms and refusing any help.

Her gift, she had said, and his taking. When she pinned his hands against the earth and told him that she was in charge he had allowed it, the sky above and the meadow beneath.

She did not let him come until the sun had fallen almost to the horizon, the tension in him stretched to the full ache of friction, a thin hot pain of need.

And then she had taken each of his nipples between her nails and pinched. Hard. Jarring.

He had climaxed as he never had before, emptying himself into her, wave after wave, involuntary, uncontrolled. And she had taken him in, wanting his seed, drawing him up as the final gift of the day. He felt the undulating motion of her insides around him and knew without a shadow of doubt that he could love her. For ever.

On their return to Saint Estelle the tavern keeper was full of the news of a group of men who had come into the town looking for two strangers.

'The leader was a big man with dark-brown hair and a scar across his cheek. Here.' His fingers drew the shape of a crescent. 'He appeared very angry.'

Lebansart. Cassie drew in her breath and knew that Nathanael had felt her fear.

'Did they say where they were going next?'

'They didn't say and I didn't ask, but they

left Saint Estelle before the noon hour and there was no talk of a return.'

'We will stay here then for a few days longer.' Nat dug into his jacket pocket and pulled out a handful of coins. 'If they should return at any time at all, I would like to be told of it.'

'Who exactly is this man, Sandrine?' The question came a few moments later when they were once again back in their chamber.

'Guy Lebansart. He was an acquaintance of Anton Baudoin.'

'What does he want?'

She shrugged her shoulders and turned away. *Me.* She almost said it, almost blurted it out before biting down on the horror. The document she should never have read shimmered in her memory.

Cassandra spent the morning at the school at Holborn. Kenyon Riley arrived around midday and walked into her office.

'Is Maureen here, Cassandra?' His voice was tinged with the accent of the Americas, and he sounded happy.

'She went to run an errand in town. I should not imagine that she will be long.'

'You look busy.'

Cassie observed the large pile of papers that littered her desk. She tried to be organised, she really did, but with the amount of work she had, such a thing was never easy.

'My sister told me the good news about your betrothal.'

'Did she? I was wondering if she would ever get around to mentioning it to anybody else.' His smile was wide.

'Reena is more contented than I have ever seen her.'

'She deserves to be.'

'I agree and I don't think she could have chosen more wisely.'

He watched her, his dark eyes perplexed. 'And what of you, Cassandra? Is there someone in your life, too?'

'You have been listening to rumour, I think?'

'More than rumours. Lord Christopher Hanley, your uncle's friend, claims he saw you in Whitechapel with Lord Lindsay. A large section of society is heeding him.'

'Well, I have never played a big part in the life of the *ton* so it will suit me to be even more reclusive. What can they do, after all?'

'Believe me, attack is the best form of defence. Come with your sister and me to the Forsythe ball and stare the naysayers down.'

'Apart from sounding risky, did you consider the possibility you might be ousted because of your association with me?'

He laughed. 'My uncle is one of the richest men in England and he is dying. No one would chance offending the next heir to the dukedom.'

In that moment Kenyon Riley seemed more like Nathaniel Lindsay than he ever had before. Powerful. Certain. Unafraid.

Perhaps he was right. Cassie had already flouted convention with the keeping of her maiden name and no true proof of her being at Brown Street existed anywhere save with Lord Lindsay. She did not believe that Nathaniel would abandon her as she had him in Perpignan.

'Maureen is having a fitting for a new gown this afternoon. You should go with her for you have worn the shades of mourning for all the months that I have known you. Perhaps it is time to branch out and live a little?'

'You sound just like Reena.'

'If I do, it is because I care about you and

because Lindsay is a good man, an honourable man.'

She nodded her head. 'I know.'

'He is also a man who would not ruin a
woman's reputation lightly.'

'He didn't.'

'Good.'

When he left her office she leaned back in
her chair and looked out over the street at the
front of the house.

Nat was indeed much more honourable than
he would think her to be, in the light of what
had happened on the outskirts of Perpignan.

They had remained in Saint Estelle for almost two weeks, always putting off their leaving for yet another day so that they could walk
to the hot pools above the village or to the
abandoned cottage on the other side of the river
and pretend that this was their house and their
life. Entwined in each other's arms, the particular glow of lovers blocked out the rest of
the world and the world became blurred and
ill defined.

Until one morning when Cassie awoke to
the knowledge that her menses had not come
and her breasts felt sore and full and heavy.

Pregnant? She counted back the days and

the weeks and always came up with the same conclusion. She was overdue and her body was telling her that things were changing inside.

Elation was her first thought and then caution. Caught out in the countryside in conditions that were hardly conducive for an early pregnancy she knew Nathanael would worry. So she said nothing.

In Perpignan she would see a doctor and then she would tell him. She knew the town and the people there. She felt at home in the narrow streets by the river. Her hand with the ruined finger crept to the secret she held in her stomach and she cradled the joy. Their child. A child born of love and of passion. Tears threatened, and she swallowed them away.

Five days later on the way into Perpignan she began to bleed. Only a little, but enough to make her understand that she needed to be somewhere quiet and peaceful, to simply stop and relax. Each morning for the past week she had felt sick on awakening and the nausea had not abated till the noon. She wanted a hot bath and a hot meal and a bed that she could stay in that was comfortable and safe.

She wanted a doctor's reassurance and the time to tell Nathanael that he would be a father, in a place where they were not looking over their shoulders for any sign of who followed them.

They had seen no trace of another since they had left Saint Estelle, always keeping away from the main roads and shadowing the rivers as they ran from the mountains down onto the plains below.

Perhaps they were safe now and whoever had been following them had given up completely. She knew Lebansart hailed from a place farther north. Had he realised the futility of chasing them and had returned home? She prayed that it might be so.

Taking the shaded alleys, they came into the outskirts of Perpignan at sunset and stopped on the left bank of the Basse River. The fortified walls stood before them and in the distance on a high citadel the Palace of the Kings of Mallorca sat, its limed walls pale in the last rays of sun.

Cassandra loved this place, with its warmth and its gentle winds off the sea. When first she had come she had been entranced to finally be able to speak the language of her mother and to feel the heat of the sun on her hair, the colours of this part of the world so different to the greyness of London.

Perpignan and the busy Mercier household had been a revelation, and the fact that she was only a cousin had made no difference to the generosity of her uncle. Celeste's mama, Agathe, had been dead a good two years so that was yet another thread that held the cousins together.

Another time.

A lost life.

A whole family gone.

She turned to look at Nathanael who sat leaning against a low stone wall, watching her.

'This was where I lived with Celeste's family. I came here to get well.'

'Hell!' His expletive was round as he stood. 'You never told me that. Would those at Nay have known of this?'

She shrugged, his anxiety seeping into her contentment. 'Perhaps they may have.'

'Then we cannot enter the town, Sandrine.'

'You think those who followed might find us here?'

'I know they will.'

The shadows around them moved in a way that was suddenly dangerous, the branches taking on the outline of shapes of men in her mind. Never again. Never again would she allow herself to be under some other person's rule.

He must have seen her fear for he moved closer. 'We will strike north tomorrow along the coast and find a ship to take us to Marseilles. I have friends there.'

She shook her head. Another trek across the countryside and with the further promise of snow. The reserves she had been storing up were suddenly no longer there and now it was not just her life she had to protect. She had to stop, the cramping pains in her stomach no longer able to be denied and ignored. 'You should leave, Nathanael. While you can. I cannot go on.'

It is me that they are after. Lebansart could pass you on a street and not know your face. Thus far you are safe.

She wished her voice did not sound so afraid, the cold air of an oncoming night making her shake. She had killed Baudoin with her knife. She could not be responsible for the death of Nathanael Colbert, too. Not him. Breathing in, she suddenly knew just what it was she must do. With all the effort in the world she smiled.

'You have bought me home and it isn't as

unsafe as you imagine. Celeste's family has a position here, a power. I can be protected.'

She should take off the marriage ring held in warm white gold around her finger and give it back, but she could not quite make herself do that. For the first time in a long while she felt virtuous.

'You cannot possibly think that a group of bandits whose secrets you know would stop pursuing you because of some aristocratic courtly authority? These people exist under far more brutal rule.'

Shaking her head, she placed one hand across his. She would go to the home of Celeste's father's best friend and his wife. She knew without doubt that they would keep her safe.

It all comes down to this, she thought, *his life and her child's safety. There was no room in any of it for her.*

The ache around her heart physically hurt as she gave in to all that she knew she must do.

'We have been flung together out of expedience and I thank you for the protection you have given me and for the things you have taught me, but…' She swallowed away the 'but' and began again. 'We are different in everything that we are and I want to go home, back to a life that I know. I am not used to such… a lack of luxury, you see, and eventually we would both feel embittered by our differences.'

Stifling grief, she looked directly at him, the stillness in him more worrying than any anger.

'Just like that?' he finally said, flatness in the words.

She nodded. 'It will be better for us both. I am sorry….' She could not go on, her hands spread in front of her gesticulating emptiness. Her smile was so tight it hurt the muscles in her cheeks.

They do not know you yet. They have no idea of exactly who you are.

'I have a comfortable life in Perpignan and I am tired of the squalor that we have needed to exist in.'

'I see.'

No, you do not see at all, Nathanael. You do not know what this is doing to my heart.

'We could meet sometimes, if you wish. I wouldn't be averse to that.'

'For what reasons, Sandrine? To demand my conjugal rights?'

She shook her head, his anger gathering in the storm clouds of his eyes. 'To reminisce.'

'Reminisce about all these weeks of memories that mean nothing to you or about the importance of material acquisitions? I think I shall say no.'

She could only guess at what he must think of her, one moment this and the next moment that. Disbelief flourished amongst fury as he lifted the blanket he slept on from his bag and rolled it out underneath a thick bush. 'We will talk again of this tomorrow when you have come to your senses. By then you may see the wisdom of my arguments and the half-witted nonsense in your own. The church, too, has strict and particular ideas about the sanctity of marriage.'

Then he simply turned away.

Cassandra's eyes felt heavy but she made herself stay awake, the moon much higher now and the true silence of early, early morning upon the grotto. They had made their beds on opposite sides of a small field of grass and he had not spoken to her again, but now he was asleep. She could hear it in his breathing and feel it in the way he had been so still for all of an hour.

She watched him from her place across the

clearing, the strong lines of his body, the dark of his hair. She could not see his face because even in sleep he had not let go of his anger and had turned away from her, the knife on a bed of leather beside him. Readied.

He would protect her to the death. She knew this. He would give his life for her without even thinking of the payment.

Her chance. To escape. Her chance to leave him here, safe against the darkness while she attempted to creep into Perpignan alone and disappear. She did not know why she had not thought that Lebansart and his men would be waiting in the one place they guessed she might have returned to.

Stupid, she chastised herself. *You knew how dangerous they were, but you did not think and now you have placed Nathanael in danger also. Mortal danger.*

Carefully, she sat up, each fraction of movement as slow as she could make it, her breath shallow and light. Then she stood, again stopping as she came fully upright, only the wind in the trees and the far-off call of a night bird.

One step and then two, the shadows taking her beneath them, blocking out the moonlight and then an open space on the banks of the

Basse, a track to a bridge across the river and
the gate on the old fortified walls. Open. It
had not been defended for hundreds of years,
a relic of a medieval past when nothing was
as safe as it was now.

She smiled at her thoughts given all that she
was running from and kept to the dark side of
buildings as she came into the town proper.
She hadn't brought her bag because she did
not want to lift it and hear the rustle of thick
canvas. But she had brought her knife, tucked
into her right sleeve in leather, the hilt extend-
ing from the thick fabric of her jacket.

Almost to the Rue des Vignes. Almost there.

Then a noise. Close. An arm snaked about
her throat, cutting off breath, and the face of
Guy Lebansart appeared next to her own.

'We thought you would come, Sandrine, although perhaps not quite so soon.'

The warmth of his palm as it caressed the
line of her cheek made her skin crawl.

Nathaniel came awake to emptiness. He
knew Sandrine was missing before he even
looked, though her bag still stood beside her
blanket.

Only a few minutes, he determined, the

wool covering still slightly warm when he checked, but the wind had come up and she had used the noise from the trees to depart.

Last night they had not spoken at all after she had told him she needed to go on alone. He swore at the absurdity of everything and the nonsense of her beliefs. Did she truly think she could just fit in again to all that she had been and forget what was between them? Had all of the past days been some kind of elaborate deception to allow her passage into Perpignan, his presence a necessary one to alleviate the sense of danger? Only that?

Nat could not believe this to be true. There were other things that she had not told him, and he needed to find out exactly what they were.

Bundling all their things together, he stuffed them into an empty space between one of the bushes nearby. He would come back for them later, but it never hurt to cover your tracks, no matter how much of a hurry you were in; spying had at least taught him that.

She would have cut along the river, he was sure of it, to cross at the next bridge. From memory the Basse had more than one bridge spanning it and was swimmable in places, though he could not see her wanting to get wet. From there she would move inwards, and the town was not so big that a good search would be impossible. No. He just had to look carefully and hope like hell that she had made the place of her destination safely.

He tipped his head, listening, but there was no sound that was different from the wind on the water and the trees, no sound that alerted him to danger or compromise. Three o'clock. The quietest hour of the night. Jogging along the track until the first bridge, he then went down on his knees.

There he had it. A fresh print in the mud showing damaged soles. She had come this way. Again he tipped his head. Now there was only the noise of the water and the first spots of rain in the wind. Tracking. His forte. He had done this so many times over so many years, following so many quarries. This time, though, the stakes were raised and he knew he had to be very careful.

'What was in the document, Sandrine? The one Baudoin wanted me to see? Pierre said that he saw you reading them.'

'I do not remember.'

'Liar.' There was an unexpected laughter in Lebansart's voice as if they were playing a game that he liked. The taste of fear and panic was bitter in her throat, but there was something else again. Triumph, if she could name it. They had not mentioned Colbert at all.

Guy's voice was close as he loosened her hair. 'Perhaps you might tell me when we are alone, *ma chérie*?' His fingers digging into her arm belied his nonchalance and around him others lingered. More than a few others. Ten or twelve, she supposed, and behind them in the shadows more would be waiting.

'Silver-tongued Leb', he was called back at the compound. A man who spun a web around his prey without fuss or contretemps. He had not even drawn his own knife, leaving that to those about him, their sharp blades seen against the dimness.

She had lost. She had rolled her dice and lost. But she had kept Nathanael safe and away in the arms of sleep.

The commotion started as a low roar and then a louder clatter. The sound of a neck breaking and a knife jammed into breath and he was there, beside her, reaching out, the touch of him breaking her heart.

Nathanael. Already the others were circling behind him, quiet in the early dawn, like a pack of wolves waiting for the command to attack.

She did not let him speak; one word and they would kill him. One wrong sound and it would all be over.

Instead she got in first, swinging her left hand around to his face and opening his jaw with the sharpened edge of her marriage ring at exactly the same time another hit him from behind, the sound of metal against his skull crunching.

He bent over, shaking his head as he did so, trying to find vision.

Do not speak, Nathanael. Do not claim me.

She thought quickly. Lebansart had ties with the government that he would not wish to jeopardise. 'I have seen him before. He is a soldier of France so better to leave him alive. But do as you will, I really don't care.'

Looking away, she tipped her head towards her captor, trying to bring forth all of her womanly powers. If they killed Nathanael she would die as well, but the threat of the might of the military seemed to have done its job.

'We don't need the army after us. So blind-fold him and bring him along.'

Another thump against flesh and she turned back, the blood from his jaw spilling over his shirt and his lips red raw from a wallop. He looked dazed, barely conscious. No blades though, no telltale sign of an injury that he would not recover from.

She laughed in relief, the sound bringing the attention of Lebansart back to her before he had the chance to change his mind. 'Perhaps we might find a place to speak, Guy.'

When his arm threaded round her and his hand cupped her breast she simply snuggled in.

'Sandrine, the whore.' She heard the voice of a man behind and knew that Nathanael would have known exactly what she allowed.

A whole lifetime of his years for a few moments of her shame. A tenable payment. She did not look back again as Lebansart led her away, his fingers closing in around the small shape of her ruined hand.

Nat came awake in a bed and a room, a priest at his side and the light of morning on his face.

'Finally you have woken, *monsieur*. You

were found beside the river Basse six days ago and have been in and out of consciousness ever since. In truth, we did not think that you would survive, but we prayed and God has answered us our call.'

Six days.

Sandrine would be long gone.

His head ached and his sight seemed compromised. The wound on the side of his jaw smarted, and he put up his hand to feel it.

'We stitched it and it is healing.'

Sandrine. He remembered the look on her face as she had led the Frenchman away. Pleasure. Flirtation. Relief. She had not even glanced back at him as she allowed the enemy everything.

Sandrine the whore.

He hated her, this woman who was his wife, hated her lies and her easy betrayal. He had not known her at all in the days of their flight from Nay. A stranger. A harlot. A cheat.

'There is someone waiting for you outside. He is an Englishman and he would like to talk with you. Do you feel up to this yet?'

When Nat nodded the priest rose and left. A moment later a tall man with sandy hair came through to stand beside the bed.

'I am Alan Heslop,' he said quietly, 'from the British Service, and I have come to see what you know of the Baudoin brothers. It seems you were at their compound and a fight ensued? I ask this of you because two of our agents were targeted and killed this past week, brothers whose names were on the letters taken by the Baudoins from the overturned carriage of Christian de Gennes. Letters that were known to have been in the compound.'

Didier and Gilbert Desrosiers were dead? Sandrine would have seen the documents and told of them, then. He stayed silent.

'My sources say there was a woman. A woman was reputed to have been there.'

He opened his mouth and then closed it. Even now, after all that had happened, he could not bring himself to betray her. If the British Service had word of her involvement they would hunt her to the ends of the earth. Garnering breath, he tried again.

'I saw no one. I left after Anton Baudoin shot me.' Lifting his shirt, he noticed the heightened interest of the newcomer. 'By all accounts, de Gennes's letters were at the compound, but I could find no trace of them.'

'Did you speak with Baudoin?'

'No. I was there in battle and there wasn't a chance of conversation before I killed him.'

'I see. You will start back for England next week. The Home Office has made arrangements for you to travel by ship, though I suppose you will need to answer more questions when you return.'

'Of course.'

'But for now you must rest. I will have warm broth sent in from the kitchen for you have lost a good deal of weight from the beating you received. It seems you were dropped in the river to drown, but your coat snagged on a pillar as the current took you away and a group of youths found you.'

'A lucky escape, then.'

'Perhaps.' The man's glance caught his own and without another word he left the room.

When he was gone, Nathaniel began to take stock of the wounds he had incurred. A heavily bandaged head, a broken right arm and two eyes that were so swollen it was hard to see.

Sandrine Mercier had betrayed both him and England to save herself.

Closing his eyes, he shut everything out and willed himself to survive.

On returning home, Nathaniel went straight

to the family seat. His grandfather, the Earl of St Auburn, stood before him, a heavy frown upon his brow.

'A further scrape that you have no explanation for, and a newly made scar on your chin that looks like you have been in another fight. And to top it all off you have lost your grandmother's ring. An heirloom. Irreplaceable. I am almost seventy-three years old, Nathaniel, and you have never stopped disappointing me.'

Nat stood and finished his drink. It had been a bad idea to expect that William Lindsay might have welcomed him home after hard, long and lonely months abroad. Tonight, however, with the portrait of his father upon the wall above his head, Nat had had enough of such hostility.

'I shall be at Stephen Hawkhurst's for the next few weeks before going back to Europe, William.'

'Running away as usual. The St Auburn inheritance does not simply see to itself, you know. A small interest on your behalf as the one who will inherit the responsibility would not go unnoticed.'

'I am certain you are quite competent at the helm. I am also certain that any changes

I made to the estate would only incense you, after all, for we have tried that track before.'

'Then take a wife, for God's sake, and settle down. You are old enough to be giving the estate some assurance of longevity, some hand into the future.'

A wife.

Nat almost laughed. He had a wife already and if he could have produced Sandrine Mercier at that moment he would have dearly loved to, if just to see the look of horror and disgust in his grandfather's eyes. But she had been lost to him in Perpignan, gone into the ether of betrayal, a woman who had not given trust a chance and who had flouted every principle of integrity.

Placing the glass carefully down on a small oak table beside him, Nathaniel tipped his head in parting and left the room.

Chapter Seven

Cassandra Northrup had come to the Forsythe town house on Chesterfield Street with her sister and Riley, just as Nathaniel had hoped she would not.

Tonight she had forsaken the colour of mourning and adorned herself in muted gold, like a flag of defiance, her eyes shining with fight. With her hair dressed and the gown complementing the sleek shades, she was the embodiment of all that Albi de Clare had once predicted.

Unmatched.

Original.

The girl in southern France only just seen through the woman she had become.

She neither fidgeted nor held on to her sister

or Kenyon Riley for support, but stood there, chin up.

He doubted he had ever seen her look more beautiful than at this particular moment and when her eyes finally met his, Nathaniel knew without a shadow of doubt that the swirling rumours of a relationship between them had reached her ears.

Her sister appeared less certain, but Riley, positioned in the middle of them both, gave the impression of a cat who had just been offered a bowl of cream. Nat wanted to hit him.

'Let the games begin.' Hawk was hardly helping matters, and Reginald Northrup to one edge of the room was watching Cassie intently, as was Hanley.

Undercurrents and anticipation. Nat did not make any move towards the Northrup party whilst he waited to see what would transpire.

The older Forsythes reacted first, moving from Kenyon Riley to Maureen Northrup without a glance at the one beside them. Then Lady Sexton and her husband turned their backs. A cut direct from a woman who was known for her own dalliance was hardly lethal. But it was the next snub that did it.

Lydia Forsythe, the young hostess who had

the most to thank Cassandra for given her recent brush with the chandelier, simply stood,
right in front of her, the slender wine goblet
she held tinkling to the ground, shattering into
pieces.

The band ceased playing.

Silence descended, the inheld breath of a
hundred guests slicing through movement,
ruin taking the physical form of a woman in
a glorious gown and sharp blue-green eyes.
She stood very stiffly, the horror of all that
was transpiring barely hidden upon her face,
her mutilated fist tight wrapped in the folds of
her golden skirt.

Despite trying not to, Nathaniel moved forward, the only motion in a room of stillness
and those all around craned their necks to see
just exactly what might happen next.

'Unfortunately, Miss Lydia Forsythe is a
woman prone to histrionics,' he said as he
reached Cassie, then he lowered his tone.
'However, if you act as if you do not care you
might be able to salvage something of the evening yet.'

Cassandra was silent, dumbfounded, he
supposed, by the way things had plummeted

from bad to worse. Worry had furrowed a deep frown in the space between her eyes.

'The trick in it is to converse as if you have all the time in the world or at least smile. Your face at the moment suggests you believe in the ruin of your name and this is exactly what others here have come to see.'

To give Cassie her due, she did try, the glimmer of humour showing where before only a frown had etched her brow.

Her sister, however, picking up the undercurrents, began to help, droning on about the seasonal changes and the new buildings in Kew Gardens. Riley stood silent, the grin on his face infuriating.

'I always love the Palm House, of course, but I think the Water Lily House will be every bit as beautiful. They say when it is finished the giant Amazonian lily will flourish within it and that a child might sit on a leaf like a boat and not get wet at all. Imagine how huge it will be.'

Amazonian must have been a difficult word to say for someone who could not hear properly, Nat determined, though Maureen's unusual pronunciation did have the effect of making Cassandra's lips turn upwards.

Around them the silence was beginning to change into chatter, the terrible scene that some might have hoped for fading into something unremarkable. Even Lydia Forsythe had pulled herself together, her mother signalling to the band to begin to play again and the young hostess making an overture of civility towards the Northrups in the form of a genuine smile.

A waltz. Without waiting for another moment, Nat asked Cassie for the dance and they stepped on to the floor.

'Thank you.' She held him away as they moved, a large space between them, circumspect and prudent. They did not dance as lovers might, though beneath his palms the warmth of the old Sandrine lingered. He tried to ignore it.

'Your uncle appears to welcome the demise of your name.'

'I think his enmity has something to do with his relationship with my mother.'

'It was his friend Hanley who told the world he saw us together.'

Her direct glance faltered. 'I have heard.'

'What would Reginald Northrup have to gain by discrediting you?'

She shook her head. 'Not the title, for Rodney is the heir apparent.'

He might have asked of her movements after Perpignan then, just to see what she might tell him, but the colour in her cheeks was returning. Besides, the middle of a crowded dance floor was not a place he wanted to hear an answer in.

'He is far more wealthy than my father, so money cannot be a factor.'

'A man with no obvious motive is more dangerous than those who have one, and if your nocturnal wanderings are known to him then it would be wise to be careful. Or cease altogether.'

She tipped her head, her expression puzzled, and his fingers tightened around hers in a will all of their own.

He was so beautiful and so known.

The corners of Cassie's heart squeezed into pain as he watched her, grey ringed with just a touch of dark blue. In his arms, here in the middle of a crowded ballroom, she felt completely safeguarded, even given the poor start to the evening. No one could touch her. No one dared. The exhilaration was surprising.

'Come with me next time, Nathaniel. Come and see just what it is that the Daughters of the Poor do.'

His lazy smile was lethal. 'I have already discovered some part of it in the bawd house off Whitechapel Road.'

'No. Not that. It's the successes you need to see.' She thought of the toddler Katie, her injuries fading and her smile blooming again. It was these things that she wanted him to know of. A new beginning. Another finer path away from the chaos that had once consumed them.

'Please.' She did not wish to beg, but this moment might be her only chance to make him understand that sometimes with endeavour honour could be reinstated.

'When?'

The anger in the room and all her problems melted away with that one small question. He would allow her a chance? For the first time that night her breath was not tight and the beat of her heart quickened from something other than fear.

'As soon as I know I shall send you word.'

'Very well.'

'Wear black.'

Nothing now was the same between them

as it had once been, but inside of her a bright warmth bloomed. The papers that held them together had probably long been lost and she no longer had his ring, but there it was, that same feeling from France that pulsed in every part of her body.

Love me. Love me. Love me.

Just a little. Just a bit. Just enough to allow the possibility of an understanding and forgiveness.

'How long has your charity been running for?' His question cut through all her fantasies.

'Two years now. I found two young girls wandering in Regent Street and on enquiry discovered they had been brought in from the country and then lost.'

'So you took them home?'

'Actually, no. I found out the place they had been stolen from and returned them. That was how it all began. Sometimes, though, it is not so easy. Sometimes young women are lost to us or put to work in the seedy houses of London and it is hard to recover them again. The only real chance of saving anyone is finding them before they are sold.'

'That sounds difficult.'

'It is. People do not want to know that this

is happening. Here in the grand salons of London they turn the other cheek because looking would be too harsh upon their sensibilities, and if Lydia Forsythe almost swoons away on seeing me, imagine what might happen if she were to confront such a truth. It is my belief that the Victorian model of virtue strips females of the things they should be capable of knowing.'

'A fierce criticism?'

'But a true one.'

'I heard that you were in Paris after...us.'

Had he not been holding her she might have tripped, the danger of letting her guard down so very real. It was the seeing him again and gaining his help in a moment when she might have been crucified without him. Everything they had been to each other imperilled all she had become alone, and the decisions she had made after he had been dragged away by Lebansart's men influenced things again.

It was foolish to imagine they could go back to what they had once had for it was far too late for that.

'I heard that you and Acacia Bellowes-Browne have an agreement.'

The muscle in his jaw tightened. 'My grandfather's hope, no doubt. I have no wish to be married again.'

The words were underlined with a raw harshness, and Cassie had cause to believe him.

Once was enough.

The dance lost some of its appeal and she pulled back. She wished she might have been able to ask him other things, important things, things that might have led to a discussion on how he perceived her ability to look after a child. His child. She took a deep breath, smiling at her sister as she swept past them in the arms of Kenyon Riley.

'They look pleased with themselves. Riley was buying all the drinks at White's the other evening and alluding to a happy event that might be occurring in his life soon. Perhaps this is it?'

'I hope so. My sister deserves each contentment that comes her way. She is sweet and kind and true.'

'Unlike you?'

Now the gloves were off.

'If it helps at all I would do things differently if I was able to begin again.' Her eyes ran across the scar that snaked down from the side of his mouth.

Unexpectedly, he laughed. 'Do you ever think back to the days before we reached Perpignan?'

All the time. Every day. Many minutes of every day.

She stayed quiet.

'I returned to Bagnères-de-Bigorre last year when I was across the border in Spain. The high bath was still as beautiful.'

'With the witchery of steam?'

Their eyes met, etched with a memory of the place. Together, close, lost in each other's arms through all the hours of the night and day. The delight of what had been jagged through her stomach and then went lower.

'What happened to us, Sandrine?'

Loss made her look away and she was happy when the music ground down to a final halt. After shepherding her back into the company of her sister and Kenyon Riley, Nathaniel quickly left. She saw him move across to stand with Stephen Hawkhurst, interest in his friend's eyes as he glanced over towards her. It was said that Hawk was entwined with the

British Service, too, and there was more in his perusal than she wanted to see.

Raising her fan, she glanced away, the balancing act of appearing all that she was not and within the company of her sister, who positively glowed with delight, taking its toll.

Acacia Bellowes-Browne was here, too, standing next to Nathaniel with her hand lightly resting upon his arm. Cassandra heard the tinkle of her laugh as she leaned closer and saw Nathaniel's answering smile.

A beautiful, clever woman with her past intact. The bright red of her gown contrasted against the dark brown of her hair. The hazel in her eyes had had poems written of them. Maureen told her that once, on returning from a weekend away at a friend's country home, and Cassie still remembered the astonishment that the eyes of a lady might incite such prose from grown men.

She was certainly using her eyes to the best of their advantage at this moment, flashing them at Nathaniel Lindsay with a coquettish flirtation and using her fan to tap him lightly on the hand as if in reprimand for some comment he had just made. Intimate. Familiar. Congenial.

Turning away from it all, Cassandra recognised with a shock that envy was eating away at her.

What happened to us, Sandrine?

Life had happened with its full quota of repayment and betrayal. Jamie had happened, too; the responsibility of a child and the overriding and untempered love that would protect him from everything and everyone. No matter what.

'Could I have the pleasure of this next dance?' Stephen Hawkhurst stood before her, his eyes probing. 'Though perhaps I should warn you I am no great mover before you give me your reply.'

'Thank you.' She liked the quiet way he spoke. 'I, too, have not had a lot of practice at these things.'

'Then we shall bumble around together. Nat was always the most proficient dancer out of the three of us at school,' he said as they took to the floor, another waltz allowing them the ease of speech.

'The three of you?'

'Lucas Clairmont was the other, but he has been in the Americas for years now making his fortune in the timber trade. None of us have families that we could count on, you see, so the connection was strong.'

He looked at her directly as he said this. 'Adversity can either pull people together or it can tear them apart, would you not agree?'

Cassie dropped her glance. Words beneath words. Nathaniel had the knack of using this technique, too.

'Indeed I would.'

'Could I give you a bit of advice, then?' He waited till she nodded.

'Sometimes in life risks can deliver the greatest of rewards, but do not be too patient about the time allotted to reap them or you may lose out altogether.'

'I am not well received in society, sir. To-night is just a small taste of that fact. To reap anything apart from disparagement might be impossible for me.'

He laughed. 'Look around you. How many men do you see who would not take risk over the mundane, who would not say to themselves if only I hadn't played it so safe as they look in the mirror in their preparations for yet an-other night out in society in the company of manners and propriety?'

Cassandra breathed out hard. 'Do you know

anything of what went on between Nathaniel and me at Perpignan?'

'He once told me that what you did and what you said you did were two different things.'

She shook her head.

'In that he is wrong. There were others… others who died because of the mistakes that I made.'

The names of those she had consigned to the afterlife came to mind, people planted through loyalty into a land that was not their own and then murdered for their service. Aye, the world ran red with the blood of martyrs and hers had been included in that.

Lebansart.

Silver-tongued Leb.

His knife had been sharp and his words were sharper still.

Bitch. Traitor. Murderer.

Once she had been none of those things and now she was all of them, marked for anyone to see. Her penance.

She smiled through the anger and held Hawkhurst's returning puzzlement as though it were only of a small importance, a trifling consideration.

'Do you ever think, my lord, that when the

world shifts in its truths sometimes one just cannot go back?'

'Often,' he replied, 'and I believe it is a shame.' As they turned with the music, Cassandra caught the face of Nathaniel watching them, his eyes devoid of feeling.

'Cassandra Northrup is nothing like I expected her to be,' Stephen said as they stood to one side of the room beside a pillar. 'In fact, I would go as far to say that after that conversation I am half in love with her myself. But she's hiding things. Big things. You can see it in her eyes when she looks over at you, Nathaniel, and she does that often.'

Nat did not want to hear this, for the cords that had held them together had been cut so irrevocably.

'Why did she go to Paris after Perpignan, Nat? She did not arrive back in England until eighteen months after you did. Why didn't she just come home?'

Lebansart. Sandrine's face turned up to his as she had left, his hands curled into hers. He wished he did not care any more, but the days beneath the Pyrenees had defined their relationship, and he found he could not let her go.

He hadn't slept with another woman since. Not one. Just that single thought made him furious. Was he destined to be for ever trapped in his feelings from the past, unable to move on with all that was being offered now? A man for whom the holy words of matrimony meant a loyalty that remained unquestioned and unbroken.

'Well, I think it is safe to say that the youngest Northrup daughter has weathered her rocky start this evening, Nat, and I can well see why. Dressed in gold she looks like something out of a fairy tale.'

A line of young swains milled about Cassandra, though she did not seem enamoured with the fact, for her frown was noticeable even at this distance.

But Nathaniel had had enough of conjecture and, excusing himself summarily, he wound his way through the substantial crowd and out of the wide front door.

Hailing his coachman, he settled into the cushioned seats and closed his eyes. For the first time ever in his life he was at a loss as to what he should do next and he didn't like the feeling one little bit.

Cassandra Northrup threw him completely,

that was the trouble. And when he had held her in the dance all he had wanted was to bring her closer. Her scent, her eyes, the feel of her skin against his.

She was a lethal concoction of beauty, brains and betrayal, but something else lingered there, too. Vulnerability, sadness and fright. What was it she was hiding? What had happened after Perpignan?

Stephen had liked her and so did Acacia. In fact, even given the collective anger of society against her earlier in the evening, he had never met a soul who did not admire her personally, apart from her uncle.

An enigma.

And she was still his wife despite all that she thought to the contrary.

He shouldn't see her again, but he knew that he would, her invitation to accompany her at night through the back streets on her charity business too tempting to turn down. What if she was hurt? She was not strong enough to rebuff a grown man who meant business, a fact he had found out in the house in Whitechapel when he had easily subdued her.

Another thought surfaced.

She had changed in four years. He could see

it in her stance and in her eyes and in the way she had held the knife in the room on Brown Street in the darkness.

He had tried to teach her a few of his best tricks of attack in the final days before they had come down into Perpignan. The blade she had taken from Baudoin was a good weapon, light and comfortable in her fist.

'Grip hard and keep it upwards for this one.' He had turned her slightly, one foot away from each other. 'Position your body behind the knife, for if you lose concentration even for a moment you will be dead.'

'Like this?' She had taken to the lesson with a surprising accuracy, her footwork balanced and the line of her arm strong. Perhaps it was the legacy of months of being a captive, *never again* stamped into every movement.

'Being left-handed will give you an advantage because your attacker will not expect it so use this quickly before he has time to define it and go in under the arc of his forearm. Close contact negates skill to some extent so aim for the artery here on the outside of the leg. He will be protecting everything else.'

So far he had explained the rudiments in the slow motion of tutelage, but now he grabbed a stick that looked solid and stood before her. 'Try it on me.'

She shook her head. 'I can't.'

'Why not?'

'I might hurt you.'

He began to laugh, the sound echoing around the small clearing, and Nat thought right then and there that this is what it felt like to be happy, here, with a beautiful girl dressed as a boy in the mountain passes of the Pyrenees.

'You are a woman,' he managed to say when he finally found his breath, 'and I have been at it a while.'

'Why did you start?' She had lowered the blade and faced him, small curls of gold-red that had escaped her plait dancing in the wind.

'Belonging, I think.' He could not believe he had been so honest and that an answer to a question he had often asked himself should have been as self-evident. 'My parents died when I was young and after that…'

'You had trouble finding yourself.' Sheathing the knife, she came forward and wrapped her arms about him. Tight and warm. 'I was the same. After Mama it seemed as though I had no compass.'

'No true north,' he answered softly.

Her eyes fell to his lips and the smile she gave him held invitation as he brought his mouth across her own. They knew nothing of each other and everything, the truth of their bodies speaking in a way words never could, telling secrets, finding the honesty. They had been hurt and they had survived. Right now it was enough.

All he could do was to keep her safe.

Chapter Eight

The note came on the third day after the Forsythe ball.

Tonight. 11:00 p.m. Wear black.

That was it. No directions. No meeting point. He held the letter up against the light and looked at her handwriting. Small and evenly shaped, no flourish of curve or wasted embellishment. No signature.

She would come here, he was sure of it, because there was no other place that had been mooted. Perhaps she expected trouble and to give an exact location might have exacerbated it. Black clothes indicated hiddenness and the fate of the man murdered at Brown Street came to mind.

The Daughters of the Poor seemed to be involved in more than the usual charity work of supplying funds. The faces of the women found near the Thames pointed to the dangers those antagonising the underbelly of London posed. One wrong move and Cassandra could be joining them, her throat cut from one side to the other.

Swearing, he crossed to the cupboard and unlocked his guns. He would be prepared for the same force others hadn't been and if anyone crossed his path and threatened Cassandra... For the first time in a long while he felt a sense of energy and release, and a vitality that had been lost in France. His eyes went to the clock. Almost six. Five hours to wait.

He was dressed in black from head to foot as she came through his window, the effect making him appear even more dangerous than he normally did.

'We will be back well before dawn and I do not expect trouble, but if it comes then I should probably warn you that...' She made herself stop babbling by an enormous effort of will. She was nervous, of him, of being here, of Nathaniel Lindsay looking so much like he had done in the Languedoc, the battered edge of a soldier in his clothes.

'I have nothing else planned,' he drawled and smiled, the languid, beautiful smile he had given her in Saint Estelle and in Bagnères-de-Bigorre before they had made love and she had forgotten that the world existed.

Shaking her head, Cassandra tried to clear her mind of the past. The past years had been so busy with taking care of Jamie and of trying to protect others that she had barely left a moment for herself. The woman in her ached for Nathaniel's touch, even though she knew she had long since forfeited the desire for him to care.

'I have been told of a place where young women are being kept against their will.'

'Who informed you?'

'The woman who lives in a house across the road.'

'And you can trust her?'

'As much as I can trust anybody.' She hoped he could not hear the hollow uncertainty as well as she could. Last time at Whitechapel a trap had been set and she hoped that it would not be the case again tonight.

'Are you armed?'

'Yes.' Lifting the material of her sleeve, she allowed him to see the knife in a leather sheath. He was good at hiding surprise, she determined, for not a single muscle in his face changed in reaction.

'Dangerous?'

The word had her chagrin rising. 'I am not the same person you met in France and I do not wish to be either. I shall never again be beholden to another and if you want to rescind your offer of help because of such an admission then I will understand.'

'I don't.'

Swallowing, Cassie tried to regain a lost balance. She was seldom off guard with anyone other than him, her certainty coming easily and without too much thought. 'I will be in charge.' She needed to regain the lead.

He nodded.

'Good.'

Sometimes, she mused, *I do not like who I have become, this person who is hard-hearted and tough-minded.* Her thoughts went to Acacia, the beautiful woman whose eyes had had poems written about them, and she frowned.

The crossroads in life had taken her in directions that had not all been her own choice and once she had traversed some pathways there was no going back. The burning boats of chance. Ludicrous to wish for some literary offering from a man, but there it was. She did. And not just any man, either, but the one who stood before her now, his pale grey eyes shaded, dressed entirely in black.

She gathered her words in carefully. 'I do not expect trouble, but sometimes it comes anyway. If it does, I will hold you in no account for the protection of my life.'

Nat could hardly believe the detachment she laced those words with. 'Because you no longer see me as your husband?'

The rush of red upon her cheeks surprised him before she turned away, a scarlet tide rising from her throat. Not all indifference, then. Already she had opened the window and climbed through into the cold darkness.

A carriage was waiting at the end of the street, a hackney cab with a driver who did not turn to greet them, but looked straight ahead.

'I pay him well for silence,' she clarified as they got in. 'The fewer people involved in this the better.'

'Does your sister ever help you in these night-time sojourns?'

'Of course not.' Shock was inherent in every syllable.

Suddenly he understood. 'How ruined does society imagine you to be?'

He caught the deep frown on her forehead through the gloom. 'Very. Societal judgement on the moral poverty inherent in prostitution holds a power that is difficult to fight.'

'But you are trying to?'

She shook her head. 'I help those without prospects or a place to live and most of these young women see their chosen profession in very different terms than those of wealth and power have a wont to.'

Nathaniel paused, trying to understand exactly what it was she was saying. 'You condone this activity? I thought you rescued such women.'

'The Daughters of the Poor encourages financial and social independence. Sometimes the only way of doing that is to make certain that those we aid are safe in their work.'

'You help them remain on the streets?'

'As opposed to leaving them in the throes of

a fourteen-hour day inside a cold dank sweat-shop run by punitive men.'

'That, I suppose, is another way to look at it.'

'The ideal of refined and protected ladies who are not only good, but who are to know nothing save for what is good is workable only for the rich, though some might say it is repression with a different face.'

At that he did laugh because he had never had a conversation quite like this with a woman. Such discourse was freeing and he wondered how far she would take her arguments.

'You are an advocate of sex for pleasure rather than for procreation? A dangerous threat to male authority?'

'Look around you, Nathaniel. Women, making their way in the world by the use of their bodies, are a highly visible aspect of our society now. The hope of the Daughters of the Poor is to keep them unharmed.'

Her use of his name was soft and familiar and when the carriage lurched to throw Cassandra against him, his arms closed around her in a movement all of their own.

Protected. Like you were not.

The scent of soft knownness was intoxicating, a small familiarity amongst everything that was changing as the carriage hurtled through the darkness of London's poorer areas.

Cassandra smiled. Nathaniel had never been a man to step back from risk—she had seen that again and again in France, and now even after a conversation of ideas that he could not have been brought up to believe in, it wasn't debate he was offering, but comfort.

A generous man. A generous lover, too. She sat up and away from him. 'You did not marry again?'

'No.'

'You did not wish to?'

He was silent.

'I thought you might be dead after Perpignan.' Cassie tried to keep the terror from her tone.

I went to Paris to look for you, to scour the streets for every face that might have been yours. I stayed there for as long as I could manage it and even as I left I looked back.

'Lebansart's men made certain I could not call for help when they dumped me by the river. When I finally awoke I was in the com-

pany of friends and taken by boat to Marseilles.'

'But you never told anyone about me?'

He shook his head.

*'I am half sick of shadows,' said The
Lady of Shalott.*

These words went around and around Cassandra's mind, the refrain plucked from Tenny-
son as he balanced desire against reality. With
more courage she might have told Nathaniel
of Jamie and of Paris and of searching for him
ever since he was lost to her. She might have
reached out, too, in the darkness and simply
laid his hand upon her heart so that he heard
the strong beat of want and need. And reply.

But Cassie did none of these things as the
carriage drew to a halt and the seedy back-
water streets came into view—the call of the
driver, the light rain against the cobbles making everything slick-wet and the moon far behind a bank of clouds ensuring darkness.

Her world. The mirrored shadows. And beyond that the river, sludge-grey as it ran slug-
gish out to a freedom at sea; neither Camelot
nor any other kingdom of dreams.

'Be on your guard,' she whispered as they made their way on foot down an alleyway, the high and close buildings leaning in, every window hung with the remains of dirty washing flapping in a dirty breeze.

A woman met them almost instantly. 'There,' she said and pointed to a door, the paint peeled and the knocker broken. 'They have been here a few days and they are back now. I seen a tall man go in there a while ago and he has not come out again since.'

Nat pulled a knife from his boot.

'He were dressed well, too,' she returned. 'He will be in the room at the rear.' Taking a coin, their informant left, her shawl high up around her hair as she scurried off into the night.

Nathaniel looked around to make certain no one else was watching them. 'Stay behind me, Sandrine.' She had insisted that she would be in charge, but he was pleased to see that she obeyed instantly and moved to let him pass. A tall and well-dressed stranger who was up to some nefarious deed. Could this be the man the urchin by the river had spoken of? The corridor inside was narrow, many closed doors leading off it.

Raising his hand, Nat pointed at keys dangling in a door that was left partly ajar. These people were not expecting any company. They were also patently amateurs. His hopes faded.

He was inside in a moment and he knew without asking a question that the two youths before him were insignificant within the chain of command. Both were young and both were unarmed, the expressions on their faces frozen.

On a bed no bigger than a cot a young woman sat crying, her hat beside her and her hair unbound.

'Who the hell are you?'

'Will Fisher, sir,' the one nearest to him stammered, 'and this is my brother. He was stupid enough to believe the Lytton gang might pay him a sovereign for a girl new in from the country and he brought her here. Now that I have talked some sense into him we don't know what to do with her.'

'Is this right?' He addressed this query to the girl and she nodded. 'Did they hurt you?'

'No, sir.'

'Why did you bring her to this place?' He addressed this question to the older brother.

'Kyle Lytton uses it as a hideaway. Jack saw them here over the past few days and thought they were still about.'

'How old are you?'

All three answered at once. The brothers were seventeen and eighteen, respectively, and the girl but fourteen.

'Get out.' This was said to the brothers and they did not tarry for a moment, moving past with the look of felons unexpectedly excused from the gallows.

Cassie was already at the girl's side. 'So you are not hurt in any way?'

'No, ma'am. The coach was late and they only just brought me here. Or the younger one did. His brother was furious and arrived straight away after.' She burst into loud and noisy sobs. 'And now it's dark and I don't know where to go or what to do…and Da will be furious if I arrive back again with nothing in me hand…' At that thought she could barely carry on.

'What is your name?'

'Sarah Milgrew, ma'am.'

'Well, Sarah, you can stay with me tonight and tomorrow we will find you a place. We have our carriage outside on the next street.'

'I canna afford much for a room, ma'am, but I can sew like an angel, Miss Davis says, and am quick with it.'

'A useful trade and most sought after.'

'My sister came to London some weeks ago and we have not heard from her again. I had hoped to try and find her.'

Nat's mind went back to the two girls pulled from the river. 'Did you sew for her?'

He saw Cassandra's eyes fasten on his face, a small frown building on her forehead.

'I did, sir. She left with one of my dresses on and another in her bag. She said she would show people what I do here and find a room for both of us. Da took her to the coach up to London and we had no word after that.'

Both the girls from the river had been well attired, but there was a touch of the country about them. Could this be the lead that he was after?

'And the coach comes into…?'

'Gracechurch Street, sir. It's five hours' travelling in good weather from Wallingford and more if it is wet. That's where the young man met me and said he could help, but when he brought me here I was afeared…' She clutched her small bag tightly and looked around the room, drab and furnitureless save for the bed.

What connection could these girls have with a man who was obviously from London? Could something have happened in their home town to lead them to each other?

Wallingford was just outside Reading. He filed the name in his mind to be considered later, but right now he wondered how often Cassandra Northrup took it on herself to bring girls like this one home. Many times he surmised by the ease in which she gathered her up and showed her through the door.

In the carriage the young woman seemed to fold into herself and lean against the far corner, a pose which spoke of hopelessness, implying the difficulty of all she had been through. But at least they had arrived in time. Observing Cassandra's care, Nat knew that circumstances had not been anywhere near as lucky for her.

The same awareness that he had experienced back in France all those years before wound into the middle of his chest, and he forced it down. These thoughts were nonsensical because he had no place in her life now, nor she in his.

He felt anger as she raised her eyes to look

at him, the street lamps illuminating the deep shadows of dimple in her cheeks, and was glad to see the gates of the Northrup residence when they came into sight, the fat-bodied hawks on each side swathed in vines.

As the carriage stopped the front door was thrown open and two maids hurried down the stairs to greet them. They had done this before, Nat thought, as Miss Milgrew was dispatched without fuss or bother into their capable hands, the trio then disappearing up the wide front staircase and into the house.

Cassandra was still sitting in the carriage, but had moved on to the seat opposite, pulling the door closed in a way that suggested she required privacy.

'If your estate or town house has any need of competent staff, we have a number of girls I could recommend who could well do with a job.'

This was the last thing he thought she might say, though as he leant forward he had to stop himself from drawing closer.

'Accompany me to the Herringford ball next week, Sandrine.'

'Why?'

'Because I want you to.' And he did. Desperately.

'Acacia Bellowes-Browne may object, my lord, and the rest of society will almost certainly be astonished.'

'You would let that worry you?'

'I try to stay out of the notice of others. I have limited the occasions that I come into the public sphere and the two times I have done so lately have both been difficult.'

'Society does not quite know what to make of you, which could be a bonus if you use it wisely. I am certain that your charity would benefit.'

'I am not so sure. The Daughters of the Poor relies on the generosity of those of wealth to give donations towards ruin without ever having to confront it.'

She always surprised him, he thought, always made him feel alive in a way he seldom had been in years. Her dimples. Her hair edging her face in curls.

'I can protect you.'

His words fell into the silence as she pushed the door open and escaped outside in one fluid movement. Once there she stopped and spoke quietly.

'I can protect myself, Nathaniel, but I thank you for your help tonight.'

But he did not leave it there. 'If a ball is too public, come to a private dinner, then, and tell me why I should make a donation to your endeavours.'

'I am certain that would be most inappropriate...'

'A hefty donation...' he added when she still hesitated.

'Very well.'

'A carriage will be sent for you the day after tomorrow at eight.'

She nodded quickly and then she was gone, pacing towards the front stairs of the Northrup mansion with the singular purpose of retreat. He watched her until the door shut and her shadow flitted briefly against the thin curtains of the downstairs salon.

My God, she should have declined his invite, she thought as she gained her room and leaned against the doorframe. She ought to be downstairs in the room off Alysa's laboratory, helping the others settle Miss Milgrew in for the night, but she could not risk letting anyone see the panic that was making her hands shake and her heart beat faster.

Nathaniel Lindsay made her careless and he made her feel things that she should not: warm things, hopeful things, things that held her both in thrall and in fear. Running her fingers across her brow, she felt the clammy sweat of dread. None of these hopes were for her and to imagine that they were would be to simply ruin everything that was.

She had a life, a good life, a worthwhile life. In the past years she had managed to find a way through adversity and to experience... contentment.

Cassie smiled at the word. Contentment. To anyone else such an emotion might be perceived to be a bland and worthless thing. But to her it was everything; a way forward, a light after the darkness and the beacon that called her on each and every day. After Nay part of her had shrivelled up and died and after Perpignan joy was an emotion she thought never to know again. But she had known it with Jamie, holding him close against her breast in Paris where she had delivered him at night, the cold fear of aloneness failing to douse the warmth and love she was consumed with.

Jamie had allowed her a purpose, a new beginning, a way back.

And now here in London all these years later another chance was being offered. Nathaniel had held her in the carriage as if he would like to offer more than a donation, but she did not dare to believe in such a promise. Not yet. Not now. Not when anyone on seeing father and son together would realise that there was no question of paternity.

The risk of everything had her sitting, her head between her legs, trying to find the breath she had forgotten to take.

'I can protect you.'

What did Nathaniel mean when he spoke of protection? The protection of marriage? The protection of being a mistress? The protection of lust and need translated into the flesh, a transient and momentary connection that would wither as soon as he saw the marks upon her breast.

Traitor.

No man could want to make love to an embodiment of betrayal. Not even one who had seen her before, whole and beautiful.

She crossed to the mirror, making certain that the door catch was on before she undid the buttons on her shirt. The cuts stood out, dark red against pale, three long slices of agony.

Lebansart's legacy.

'Tell me what was in the documents, Sandrine. Tell me and live.'

She had recited the names without further hesitation: her child's safety or that of two faceless men whom she had never met? There was no real struggle, a fact that she was to relive over and over in nightmares that wouldn't fade. She had stood there with the blood from her breast sticky against her fingers and she had itemised all that she had seen.

He wrote her words carefully in a book with a brown leather binding and a quill whose feathers had seen better days. The ink had stained his finger with black. Little details. Remembered. Her voice had shaken as she spoke.

'Good. Very good. You were worth the trouble.' Those were his words as he had left the room.

Leaving her to die, slowly, from a loss of blood. But he had no notion that she was her mother's daughter and that she would know exactly what to do to lessen the flow and survive. A heavy wad of sheet and two long belts wrapped tight across them before lying face down on the thick mat and willing herself out of panic.

Survival. She breathed as shallowly as she could and tried not to move at all. And then after a few more hours she began to feel less lightheaded and warmer, the quilt she had heaped upon herself an added comfort and the noon-day light at the window spilling across her.

It had taken her another hour to find the energy to leave the room and make her way into the street. A doctor on a visit to a patient had found her and bundled her into his carriage and after that she struggled with living for a very long time.

Except for Jamie. Except for the growth of a child, Nathanael's child, the only thing anchoring her to the world as everything spiralled into despair and hopelessness.

Her uncle's friend had bought her a ticket to Paris as soon as the fever left out of respect for the Mercier family. He had arranged for his small house in Montmartre to be opened for her and sent two maids and a butler along to help her in her quest for independence.

She did not mention her pregnancy and allowed him no notion of her own family back in London. She needed to think and to plan. She needed to find Nathanael if she could and she needed to be well away from Lebansart.

The house was quiet and situated in a street not far from the Sacré-Coeur, with a view across the rooftops of the city. Even with the beauty of white marble washed in rain she was lonely and sad, shock reaching into the depths of her soul.

And then one day whilst sitting in a park, wrapped warmly against the capricious springtime winds, a colourful bird had come to sit on the branch of a shrub in front of her and her baby had moved.

Life returned. Hope blossomed. The want to survive overrode the desire to simply cease to be, and she recovered.

Rebuttoning her shirt, Cassie looked back at herself in the mirror. No longer as thin. No longer as sad. No longer hobbling into each successive hour with the burden of betrayal heavy on her shoulders. The Daughters of the Poor had given her life a purpose and Jamie had given her body a heart. She could not endure uncertainty again. If she went to Nathan-

iel's dinner tomorrow night she would tell him
she couldn't.

It was that simple.

Chapter Nine

Nothing was simple.

Nathaniel was dressed down tonight, his clothes less formal, the unbuttoned white collar of his shirt bold against the dark of his skin, a loose garment that gave him a sense of danger and familiarity. Cassie knew that it was more than scandalous to come to his house at night and alone, but both want and need had brought her here. Shaking away doubt, she moved inside. She was not about to give in to the narrow confines of Victorian rules, and besides, in the eyes of God they were married.

'I am glad that you came.'

His house was well appointed, every piece of furniture in sight beautifully wrought. Because she was so nervous she picked up a small bowl on a side stand, admiring the colourful flowers that marched around the rim. It was the one thing that did not look eminently English.

'I remember these designs from the marketplace at Perpignan. I always liked them.'

His eyes today were the shade of well-worn slate and warmer than usual. She wished he had been plainer, less intimidating and wished, too, that she might have worn some other dress than the one she had on, the starched blue silk too grand and stiff for this occasion.

'I have a fire going in the middle salon and some white wine.'

Nodding, she followed him. The fire sounded inviting though she was determined to refuse any drink at all. *Keep your wits about you*, she said to herself, *and understand that he will want explanation of what happened in Languedoc.*

The new room was more imposing than the last. A rich floral carpet was laid on the floor, the deep colour in it matching the heavy curtains at the windows. All around every wall mirrors and pictures abounded and, as in his library, there were shelves of books stacked almost to the ceiling. A generous fireplace blazed at one end and it was here that he led her. Two leather seats had been positioned opposite each other, a small table between them with fluted glasses upon it.

The apprehension of being here was growing by the second. A portrait of a woman in full riding regalia graced the nearest wall, and when he saw her looking he smiled.

'My mother loved horses.'

'She was very beautiful.'

'Indeed.' The talk then tailed down into silence, a thousand other things to say beneath the polite banter and no way to voice them.

I love you. I never stopped loving you.

For one horrible moment Cassie thought she had blurted the words out, bare and naked in their truth, and shock crawled up her spine, caught in the gap of honesty.

'Please, do sit down.' He waited until she complied before doing so himself, pouring two drinks and placing one before her. 'How is Miss Milgrew settling in?'

A different topic completely and one she was pleased to speak of. 'Sarah has been a godsend and has begun teaching the other girls the fine art of sewing.'

'Is there any sign of the sibling?'

'No. It seems she has quite disappeared. You

asked if she sewed for her sister the other night and I thought the question odd. Why was that?'

'The bodies of two young women were pulled from the Thames a month back and no one claimed them. Both were dressed in finely sewn gowns.'

'You think it could be her lost sister, then? I see.'

'Do you, Sandrine? Do you see how searching out the damaged women of London may have more consequences than you can imagine? One day you could end up in the river yourself.'

'I take every precaution…'

'And you think that is enough against an opponent who is bigger and stronger than you.' He no longer sounded as mellow. In fact, now when she caught his glance she looked away quickly, so much of Nathanael Colbert before her. The soldier. The lover. The man who had watched her betray him, blood running down his chin.

'Where is the Colbert part of your name from?'

'It is a lesser title of mine. The St Auburn earldom contains many and as the heir I have an entitlement to them.'

'A real name? Not made up?'

'Made up like Sandrine Mercier was, you mean?'

'My cousin Celeste often called me Sandrine and Mercier was her surname.'

'I know. I went back and spoke to what was left of the family. An uncle, Gilles Mercier, informed me of the demise of Celeste and her father, though he said nothing of you.'

'Celeste had that knack of making everyone around her look invisible.'

'Or you barely went out?'

This was running too close to the bone. Depression had kept her in bed for a long time, but she did not wish to recall that.

Even sitting, the breadth and height of Nathaniel Lindsay was substantial. She remembered how she had loved his largeness after the small men of Languedoc. She remembered his scent, too, an evocative mixture of plain soap and maleness.

'Your sister visited me last week. Did you know that?'

'Maureen came here?' She could not keep her astonishment at bay.

'She wanted to be assured that I was not threatening you in any way. She stood her ground and cautioned me that she would not tolerate anything that may hurt you. When I told her that I had pretended to bed you in order to help you from being discovered and compromised, she was happy.'

More unspoken words shimmered in the chasms.

Were pretence and lies all that once held us together?

Here it was harder to maintain the falsehood, even with the arguments Cassie could muster for carrying on with such a charade. She felt a choking want in the back of her throat and swallowed it down. The wine helped, a fine dry white that gave her hands something to fidget with and her mind something other than him to dwell upon. But secrets could be as damaging as any wound and her fingers tightened around the crystal glass.

All of a sudden she wished he might just reach out and take away choice. She wanted the feelings she had discovered in Saint Estelle and in Bagnères-de-Bigorre here in London, in the quiet warmth of his beautiful house, far away from others and from the responsibility of her everyday life.

Nathaniel made her believe in fantasy. That

was it. He had before in southern France and he did again now, the muted sounds of the city far away and the clock showing eight-thirty in the evening. Still early. The blue in her gown shimmered as she shuffled back and sat up farther.

'My sister feels it is her duty to protect all those about her.'

'Then such obligation must run in your family.'

At that she laughed. 'Perhaps it does in Maureen, but Papa is too busy with trying to understand the complexities of science and my other sister Anne is too preoccupied with her brood of children.'

'There is also a brother?'

'Rodney. He is the youngest.'

He had told her once that he was without siblings.

Alone. The word came with a forcefulness that made her blink. He was still like that; the solitary detachment of one who was careful not to anchor himself to another for fear of being disappointed. Oh, how well she knew that feeling.

The clock in the corner boomed out a further passage of time, and Nathanael finished his first drink and poured himself another, eyeing hers as he did so.

'You do not like the wine?' he commented.

She looked nervous and her hand shook as she made herself take a drink. Not just one sip, either, but three. Fortification. He wondered perhaps whether it had been a bad idea to invite her here because the ease that had always existed between them seemed dissipated tonight into a sheer and utter nervousness, her eyes skirting away from his and her body ramrod straight.

'Albi de Clare is of the opinion that you and Maureen are two of the most beautiful women in London.'

She smiled. 'Is his eyesight hampered, my lord?'

'Many I have spoken to would agree with him. But they also say you are prickly and distant to any advances that come your way. Most make a point of telling me that you in particular seldom venture out to partake in any of the entertainments that most are fond of.'

'There are other things that I need now more than a man, Lord Lindsay.'

He reached out and stroked a finger down

the soft skin near her wrist, measuring the beat when he had finished. She often wore gloves, the left-hand fingers specially fashioned so as to show no signs of her old injury.

'Indifference requires a less rapid pulse, *Sandrine.*'

Cassie did not pull away, but watched his thumb as it moved up her arm and he had the sudden and unexpected thought that she might allow him more.

'I would like to know you again as I did once.' Firelight was reflected on the smooth skin at her throat and it was now there that his touch lingered.

'No. It cannot be as before.' She said the words slowly, enunciating each one, and he did not quite understand what she meant.

'Before?'

'Only a kiss. Nothing else.'

God. His body leapt with her words, shock warming everything. She did not turn away, but met his glance full on, the depths of burning need and pain inside them making his breath catch, for the Sandrine of old was so easily seen.

New secrets lingered there as well, he was too much of the spy not to recognise that, but they would have to wait. For now he pulled her up towards him as he stood, the length of their bodies touching. He did not wish to frighten her or make her call a halt so he was cautious. It was enough to feel her against him, willingly fitting into the contours of his body and to smell her particular and sweet scent.

Strands of hair that had loosened from the knot at her nape lay across his arm, bright against the darkness of his clothes.

Night and day. Lost and found. Lies and truth. All were there as he brought his mouth down across hers, the limit of a kiss shrugged away by the blinding honesty of connection. They were back again in the hot pools of Bagnères-de-Bigorre and in the shadowed room at Saint Estelle, a thousand days of apartness lost into union.

No careful kiss this, after all, but a full-blooded connection of want. Slanting his lips, he brought her closer, the stark heat of his body tightening with desire. Sensation washed through reserve and instead of the judicious touch he had promised he ravished her mouth with his tongue, trying to make her understand the futility of boundaries and the depth of his need. The savage movement of years of memory and betrayal lingered there, too.

This kiss was different from any they had shared in France, the play of anger on one edge and a trace of hate. Once, as a girl, Cassie might have been frightened by such an emotion, but now she relished it, the woman in her responding to their complex and circuitous layers of history. She wanted to punish him back, too, for not being there when she had Jamie and for the all the loneliness she had felt ever since; for the pain of his birth and the cold hard hours afterwards of isolation and solitude.

A shared and desolate despondence.

Her fingers raked across the bare skin on his neck and held him closer, the breath between them hoarse and rasping. Hardly proper. Barely kind. She wished she might tell him everything even as she knew she would reveal nothing.

But for this moment Nathanael Colbert was hers. She could not think of the earldom or of society or of the duties that would drag Lord Lindsay from her as soon as they broke off their kiss.

Nothing but now, but, oh, how she yearned

for more, his body moving inside her and that particular moment of release when all the world fell away to the beat of pleasure and purpose, the dark, hard power of sex mitigating everything.

When the kiss was finished, as she knew it must, she laid her head against his chest, feeling his heart pounding in her ear, like the beat of some song that was played too fast for the melody.

Their lives. Out of tune and spinning into chaos again.

Jamie.

She made herself stand alone. For now she needed the time to think. Her smile was false when she finally looked up at him—she knew it was, and yet it was all she had left.

'I do not think this was a good idea.'

He laughed. 'Then you have not had many other kisses or you would recognise the magic in it.'

She was pleased he did not comment on the anger.

'I am older now, Nathaniel, and wiser. What I think I want and what I need are now two different things. I cannot make a mistake again.'

'Come to bed with me, Sandrine. Now.'

Shocking. Enticing. Impossible.

'And if I did, what then? Can you honestly say that without reservation you have forgiven me for what happened at Perpignan?'

His smile faded and he remained silent. When he looked away she knew that she had lost him.

'I think I should go.'

One minute of silence and then two before he simply reached down and rang a small silver bell she had not noticed on a table. Footsteps outside could be heard immediately.

'You rang, sir.' The servant was all a good butler should be, circumspect and prudent.

'Miss Northrup is just leaving, Haines. Could you find her coat and see her out?'

'Yes, sir.'

Lord Nathaniel Lindsay did not move as she pushed past him and followed his man from the room.

He punched his hand against the hardness of the wall behind as she left and liked the pain that radiated up his arm.

What the hell was wrong with him? Why could he not have given her the soft words she was after, the oaths of forgiveness and absolution? Lebansart's face drifted into his mind and the anonymous visages of two men who had never known what was coming. The last words at Perpignan were there, too, as she had curled her fingers into those of his enemy.

Sandrine the whore.

He hated the truth of it, but he could not change. An impossible future moulded from an old and familiar hurt. How long had she stayed with Lebansart? It had been eighteen months later that she had returned to England according to Hawk. That long? A lifetime compared with the paltry weeks that they had been allotted. Lifting his glass, he finished the lot and his body ached with the loss of her.

Chapter Ten

'Lord Lindsay was at the Venus Club the night before last, Cassie, and according to our uncle he was enjoying all that was on offer there.'

Maureen gave her the information over the breakfast table the week after her meeting with Nathaniel, the anger in her voice lancing the words with repugnance. 'I would have thought him to have had more taste,' her sister added as she helped herself to a plate of scrambled eggs from a heated silver dish on the sideboard.

Cassandra was shocked, the shame that was still substantial from their last meeting now compounded by Lindsay's obvious lack of regard for women. He had sent a sizeable chit, too, with a servant the day after she had seen him. The bribe for the Daughters of the Poor now felt like a severance token, a way of apologising for a relationship that he did not want and could not pursue.

Nathaniel Lindsay was a bounder and a cheat; that was what he was, a man who would prey on the hard times of others and yet pretend an interest in her work with the Daughters of the Poor; a man without the courage to chance her offering of more than a kiss. She was suddenly glad that he had dismissed her from his company if this was what he had become, though anger and disappointment made her shake.

'Kenyon said he could not imagine Lindsay in such seedy places when he has all the women of society to choose from, but as Uncle Reg was adamant in his identification, I presume it must be the truth. Stephen Hawkhurst accompanied him by all accounts.' She stopped then, a worrying look in her eyes. 'I had hoped you and Lindsay might have been friends. I noticed him watching you closely at the Forsythe ball, and he was certainly helpful there.'

'Perhaps he feels responsible for me somehow. Lords of the peerage have an inflated view of duty towards others in need.' Cassandra prayed that her sister might take her explanation as an end point to the conversation, but she was disappointed.

'Kenyon thinks he is a good person. He also said that his grandfather is a mean-spirited old miser who needs a hearty talking to.'

'Your husband-to-be has strong opinions, Reena.'

'I know. Isn't he wonderful?'

Unexpectedly, Cassandra found herself laughing. Her sister had changed from a woman who often questioned masculine dominance to one who was allowing Kenyon Riley every right of persuasion. It was heartening because Maureen looked so very happy, a smile pinned on her lips almost permanently now and nothing and no one could dull it. Not even their father when he joined them in the breakfast room looking irritated.

'Reginald was here again yesterday and he is becoming more and more of an interfering and bombastic bore. I shall instruct the servants not to let him through to the laboratory again because he cannot help touching the experiments even when I ask him not to. Your mother was always exasperated by him and I can well see why.'

'I think he was after the watch Grandfather

brought home with him from South Africa,
Papa. He said the other week that he was certain it was supposed to be given to him.' Maureen sounded distant, as though the problems
of this household were becoming less and less
of a concern to her.

'The acquisition of family heirlooms is the
only reason he ever comes calling and Lord
knows he has more in the way of chattels than
we do.'

'Why do you give him things, then?' Cassie
joined in the conversation now, interested in
his answer.

'Because he never loved a woman like I did
or had children. Offspring. Heirs. His life is
as barren as a moor and as empty. It seems he
uses the clubs selling pleasure these days as
a reason for living. God knows he is always
trying to deter me from funding your charity.'

Cassie frowned. 'He told me at the Forsythe
ball the other week that I should be placing my
efforts into the marriage mart and that the frippery of charitable works would put any man
off an alliance with our family.'

'And yet he himself has never entertained
the idea of a bride?' Maureen's words were
laced with question.

'Oh, he did once. He asked your mother to marry him and she refused. I don't think he ever forgave her for marrying me instead.'

Cassandra had heard this before from her mama. Alysa was a woman who barely spoke of the personal, but once when Uncle Reginald had come to the door she had pretended she was out and had given an explanation for the lie. Her love of science was the reason. Reginald for all his money and handsome looks could never abide a woman with a brain and if Alysa had a goal in life it was to understand the theory behind the small and unseen badness in a sick person.

'She had a lucky escape, Papa, and I am certain she knew it.'

'But it has made him mean and smallminded.'

Their father was usually far more reticent about discussing any of his feelings so Cassie determined that he must be worried about something. She had no further opportunity to ask questions, though, as he finished his breakfast and left the table. Back to the laboratory, she thought and watched as he left, a man slightly bent over by life and loss. She hoped she would not be like that in thirty years.

A few moments later a knock on the door took their attention. These days any unexpected caller had the effect of making Cassandra's heart race wildly just in case it was Nathaniel Lindsay, but when their butler showed in Elizabeth Hartley from the school, a new worry surfaced. She looked alarmed and anxious, her more usual languid demeanour disappeared beneath a flushed face and bright eyes.

'Another girl has been pulled out of the river. We have just been informed of it and we think it may be Sarah Milgrew, for she has not returned home for two nights.'

Both Cassie and Maureen stood.

'When did you last see her?'

'She said she had to go out around six the day before yesterday and never came home. She had some information of her lost sister, it seems, and was hurrying out to find her.'

'How did the word come?'

'A young boy came to the front door and asked for her by name. When I looked in her room there was no note or anything. After we heard the news this morning, though, Mrs Wilson said I was to fetch you and that you would know what to do.'

Both sisters looked at each other. 'We will come, of course,' Cassandra said. 'Where has the body been taken?'

'To the police station in Aldwych.'

'Then I need to be there. If you stay here, Maureen, until I return we will all go to the school together.'

Twenty minutes later she was pulling up in front of the Aldwych constabulary in a hired brougham. God, how she hated what she had come to do, but as there was no one else for the job she took a deep breath and stepped down from the carriage, walking right into the path of Lord Nathaniel Lindsay.

Because her mind was on the dreadful business of the discovered body it took her a second to register his presence and react. The bloom of anger and discomfort could be felt on her cheeks.

'It is Sarah Milgrew, Cassandra. I have just identified her.' His words replaced embarrassment with a deep and shocked horror. 'Her throat was cut just like the last girls'.'

He was not being careful with his facts and for that Cassie was glad. She did not wish to be treated like a woman who would need the truth filtered and sanitised. His grey eyes were filled with the sort of anger she had seen them to contain in France.

'The constabulary said that there is nothing else that they can do at the moment. I have asked them to keep me informed of any new developments, however, and they said they would send someone over if there was other information uncovered. I have my own leads, too, that I shall want to investigate.'

'You have an idea of who it might be?'

'Sarah Milgrew's home town of Wallingford might allow us some answers. I will travel across there in the morning.'

'If you could keep us up to date, too, we would be most grateful.'

'Of course. Would you like me to drop you at home?'

'If you have the wish to.' Sadness had hollowed her; sadness for Sarah and for the other girls who had died.

'My carriage is this way.' For the first time he touched her, his hand at her elbow guiding her past a group of people walking the other way; an aloof and detached touch that was discarded as soon as they reached the conveyance. Once inside he kept talking.

'Surely someone else could have been sent from the Daughters of the Poor other than you to identify the body?'

'There are no men on the pay roll, if that is what you are suggesting.'

'Older women, then. Married women.'

The barb dug deep, lancing all the hurt and anger. 'I might remind you, Lord Lindsay, that I was married even though you seem to have forgotten the fact entirely.'

'Hardly.' His eyes ran across her body in the way of a man who remembered everything.

'Well, as someone who spends his evenings in the bosom of the Venus Club you give all the impression of otherwise.' My God, she thought as soon as it was out of her mouth. What had made her say that? The sharp edge of hurt probably and the wasted loss of hope.

His laughter surprised her. 'You think I should stay at home and read instead?'

'Rumour has it the girls there are very young.'

All humour fled. 'Enough, Cassandra. You have no idea of my reasons for being there.'

'Oh, I am certain I have, my lord. Do not all men have the same purpose once they set foot in such hallowed halls?' Her temper was at full flight now, irreversible and unstoppable as years of her own loneliness and ruin came flooding in. 'I just had expected better from you, the unwise hope of one who has made choices that come back to haunt, I suppose, and your penchant for such places makes a mockery of any history between us.'

'The history of you abandoning me in Perpignan for the arms of Guy Lebansart, you mean, and staying in Paris for the whole of the next eighteen months with him?'

'Who told you that?'

'Nobody had to. I was there, remember, as you happily went off with him. A woman who looked as though she could barely wait to be in more than his arms.'

She hit him then, full across the face, the sound in the carriage terrible and absolute. But he did not pull back. Rather, he grabbed at her shaking hand and yanked her forward, his mouth coming down on hers in a single frozen angry grimace.

And he took exactly what he wanted, bearing down with a force she could not deny. One hand threaded through her hair, tethering her to him, and the other gathering both wrists, bundling retaliation into stillness. He did not hold back either, ravaging her mouth with fury, barely allowing breath. At first she fought him, and then before she knew it another feeling altogether arose and she clung to his kiss as though her very life depended on it.

With a curse, he let her go.

'I am sorry.' He didn't sound at all like he usually did, and the scar across his chin stood out in a raised white line. Neither did he look sorry. Rather he appeared as though with only the slightest of provocation he might act in the very same way yet again.

Unbridled and rampant. A lord who was used to an easy domain over others and was trying now to find a normalcy that had never been part of their relationship together in order to survive.

'We bring out the worst in each other.' More of his words slung with insult, though a small edge of them held another emotion. Shame, if she might name it, for his behaviour and for her own, each marooned in a half place of regret.

The silence was welcomed. The clip-clop of the horses, the call of the driver, the sounds of a busy London street. Normal and proper after everything else that was not. Her lips felt rough and dry, but she did not dare to lick them in case he interpreted such an action wrongly. With eyes downcast she swallowed back tears and sat perfectly still, pleased when the horses were called to a halt and the door was opened to the Northrup town house.

The footman helped her out. Nathaniel did not touch her or look at her. It was as if three feet were a thousand miles as she climbed down onto the white pebbles.

'If I hear any other news about Sarah Milgrew I shall let you know, Miss Northrup.'

'I would be indebted, Lord Lindsay.'

The polite manners of society hung across an undercurrent of weariness and then he was gone.

White's was busy when he flung himself down on a leather wingchair opposite Hawk half an hour later and ordered himself a double shot of their strongest whisky.

'A run in with the mysterious Miss Cassandra Northrup, I presume?'

Nat ignored Hawk's jibe because the whole fiasco was just too confusing to dwell upon right now. 'Another woman has been brought out of the river.'

'Lord.' Hawk sat forward. 'Who is it this time?'

'A girl whom the Daughters of the Poor had found and given a home to. The sister of one of those dragged from the Thames last month, I am guessing.'

'Was there a meeting of the Venus Club that night?'

'No.'

'Damn.'

'But the girl had made enquiries the evening before at the Sailors Inn concerning her sister. The tavern keeper remembers her asking. I also know the name of her home town, so perhaps something happened there?'

'Bits and pieces dropping into the jigsaw. God, how I love this game.'

'I doubt the youngest Northrup daughter would see it in those terms, Stephen. She was furious to hear I had been at a meeting of the Venus Club.'

'You did not enlighten her of your true purpose?'

'And run the risk of having her poke her nose into the whole conundrum? It is getting more dangerous by the day and she seems to think she is indestructible.'

'I see your point.' Hawk leant forward and frowned. 'Have you been in a fight? Your face looks bruised.'

'Cassandra Northrup hit me. Hard.'

Stephen began to laugh. 'She makes you foolish, Nathaniel, and it's about high time that one of us found a woman who managed to do that. Besides, she is your wife.' He raised his glass and drank, his smile laconic. 'It's been years since you have given any woman the time of day and this one...' He stopped as though picking his words carefully. 'This one makes you feel again.'

Anger. Wrath. Irritation. Frustration. Helplessness. Fear. For what she was involved in and for the risks she took. Aye, Hawk was right in his summation of strongly feeling something. Nat stayed quiet.

'There is another matter that I have heard amongst the whispers of gossip, Nat, and I am not sure if this is a good time to tell you of it.'

'Something about Cassandra Northrup, you mean?'

'Yes.'

Nathaniel took a breath in because by the tone of voice that Stephen was using he knew the news was bad. 'What is it?'

'She has a son.'

The bottom fell out of his world in one dizzying and frantic sort of disbelief. Of all the things he had expected Hawk to say this was not one of them.

'How old?'

'Word is that she returned from Paris with him in tow.'

Nat's hands scraped through his hair as he tried to recover a lost composure.

Was the child his?

Anger filtered his world with a red haze, the beat of his heart drumming in his ears as he put down his glass. Had Sandrine been pregnant in Perpignan and not told him? His mind skirted back to the timings.

After his behaviour in the carriage he felt it unwise to confront Cassandra with this new question, for the answer she gave back would determine everything. He wished that he could have gone then and there to her and sworn that the parenthood of her son did not matter to him.

But he knew that it did. With care, he straightened in the leather seat.

'Is it yours?'

Stephen's voice came through a billowing

loss and for the first time in a long while Nat found himself unable to formulate even the smallest of thoughts.

Cassie held her son close against the night and listened to his breathing, the moon coming in between the curtains of patterned velvet, illuminating the bed with its paleness.

Jamie came to her room in the night with a wail of worry, another dream disturbing slumber and leaving him upset and frightened. Often she instructed his nanny to let him come to her in the early hours before the dawn if he awoke for she liked sleeping with him.

She wondered if he remembered his time in Paris, the uncertainty, the desperation. She hoped he held no recollection of her crying out for Nathanael and searching for a face that might look like his in the Place des Vosges or the busy markets of Les Halles. She had walked the length and the breadth of the city, hoping that she might see him once in the uniform of an army officer, in the Luxembourg Gardens and the Parc du Champ de Mars opposite the L'Ecole Militaire. Just to explain. At the Hôtel des Invalides she had waited on the esplanade and searched. This face and that one. Men ravaged by battle and memories, but none of them were Nathanael Colbert.

Today in the carriage she had hated him. No, she shook her head for that was not quite true. Even membership in a club renowned for its debauchery could not dull the hopes she harboured. His kiss had been full of anger, a savage punishing caress, but underneath the fury, passion simmered. She had felt it sliding beneath intent and taking root, anger compromised by lust.

Crying over the loss of Sarah before finally going to sleep and then being woken when Jamie had padded into her room in the small hours of the morning, Cassandra felt dislocated.

Life and death was entwined irrevocably and now, as the moon waned and the dawn called she knew that she would have to be honest no matter what the consequences. Jamie was a boy who needed a father and it was only right that she gave Nathaniel Lindsay the chance to get to know his son.

Their son. A child born from love and from passion.

Tears pooled behind her eyes. Jamie was the reason she had lived, a calling hope when everything else had been lost. He had looked like Nathaniel from the first moment he had been born, wise eyes staring up at her under a shock of black hair. And every single year the resemblance had grown.

Turning over, she looked at the ceiling and remembered the kiss in the carriage. She wanted that feeling again, pounded by strong emotion and rescued from the inertia that had made her feel so flat for all the months and years without him. But she could not blackmail him into loving her by offering their son as bait. No. She would have to let Jamie go and trust Nathaniel to be the sort of father she imagined he would be. Then she would need to step back. The realisation brought her arms in an involuntary protest around the small sleeping body and she dozed with him snuggled in beside her until the morning.

She would tell him as soon as she saw him next.

Nathaniel was waiting for her by his carriage outside the school in Holborn two mornings later and it seemed to her as if he had been there a while.

'I want to talk to you.' He did not bother

with the niceties of greeting, cold grey eyes levelled at her with more than a hint of anger.

'Here?'

'Perhaps the park opposite? Could you accompany me for a walk?'

A tight request, just holding on to politeness.

'Very well.'

She was unsettled by his demeanour. She had sworn to herself she would give him the truth about Jamie and yet now the thought of actually broaching such a topic made her feel sick. Today he looked nothing like the man she had made love to in the high passes of Languedoc. No, today plain fury seemed to radiate from him.

A few words and her life might be completely different and torn apart. Jamming her teeth together, she did not say a thing, watching him as he shepherded her behind a small green hedge and turned.

'Why did you take so long to return to England? From what I have been able to gather it was almost two years before you came back.'

Her eyes snapped up to his. Something had changed. He knew of Jamie. She could see it in his face and in his stillness. He always had that, a crouching sense of both calm and danger. His silence had its own voice, too. She had known this moment would come, of course, through four long years of imaginings. How often had she sat in the dead of night and wondered how this secret would be told.

'Hawk implied you had a child in France.'

Not like this. Not like this. Not asked with anger. Not out in the open where anyone might interrupt and the time to explain was not on her side. She cursed Stephen Hawkhurst for imparting the information.

'Was there a child from our union, San-drine?'

Ah, so easy to simply lie given his uncertainty, but she found she could not.

'There was. There is,' she amended and heard breathlessness in every syllable. 'Jamie is three years old and will be four at the end of next month. He was born in Paris at the end of July in 1847.' All the facts for him to place together, the answer hanging in any interpretation he wanted.

The quiet continued for one moment and then for two.

'He is mine.'

Cassie had never heard such a tone from Lord Lindsay; the hope was audible as was the shock, but it was the simple yearning that got to her.

'Ours.' She could not say more, the tears in her eyes welling with the relief of her admission.

'And Lebansart?'

The ugly name crept in to all that should have been beautiful. 'He never touched me in that way.'

Emotion was etched into every hard line of Nathaniel's face. 'It certainly looked like he wanted to from where I stood.'

'The names I gave him put paid to that. He was too keen to use the information I had recited to think of anything else. He left with his men ten minutes after you last saw him.'

'Did he hurt you?'

Turning her face away, she was glad not to see the question in his eyes. 'James Nathanael Colbert Northrup is our son's name. I could not think of another way to make sure you would know you were his father if anything was to happen to me.'

He breathed out loudly, a tremor in the sound, all other thoughts washed away. She was pleased for it.

'When can I see him?'

Cassie was quiet. She was, after all, not certain just what sort of a part Nathaniel wanted to play in his son's life. Or what kind of a role *she* might be placed into.

'Does he know about me?'

'He thinks that his father died in France. I thought that, too.'

With a curse, his glance took in the far horizon. Allowing himself time to take in the enormity of all that she had told him before he needed to give an answer, she supposed.

'Why was he born in Paris?'

A different tack. Beneath such a question other queries lingered.

'My uncle's best friend had a house there and allowed me the use of it. He sent servants to help me settle.'

'You did not think to come back to England?'

Shaking her head, she took his hand. 'I wanted to have Jamie first. I wanted to have our baby without the pressure of all that would transpire in London had I come home alone. I was sick for most of the pregnancy and I did not trust a sea journey. I also believed that I could find you in Paris and explain.'

His grey eyes sharpened. 'Did you know you were pregnant before Perpignan?'

Looking straight at him, she nodded.

His anger was immediate. 'You knew and yet you still left?'

'Much has happened since we were young, Nathaniel. Good things and bad. But Jamie is one of the good things and that is where our focus must lie.'

Relief filled her when he nodded. A relationship held by the smallest of threads, the past between them a broken maze of trust. Sandrine Mercier and Nathanael Colbert had been vastly different people from Cassandra Northrup and Nathaniel Lindsay. But each of them in their own way was now trying to find a direction.

'Where does this leave us, then?' She heard the tiredness in his words.

'If we were to be friends it might be a start.'

Friends?

Nathaniel mulled over the word, hating the limitations upon it, yet at a loss to demand more. She had borne him a son in a place far from home. Jamie. James. The word budded within him like a prayer answered.

But it was Cassandra whom he needed to

think about now. In France they'd experienced lust and passion and avidity as they had made their way through the high mountain passes. Now she needed friendship. It was what she was asking of him, this quieter calm after a storm. Friendship, an emotion he held no experience of with a woman. Did it preclude touching? He moved back, for the expression on her face looked as uncertain as his, eyes shaded equally in worry and hope.

Taking a breath, he smiled as he saw her hand shake when she pushed back the curls that had escaped from beneath her bonnet. 'Does he have hair your colour or mine?'

'Yours. I am constantly amazed that my sister does not see the resemblance and comment upon it.'

'A St Auburn, then.' The words slipped from him unbidden, and she sobered instantly.

'A piece of paper all those years ago was easy to sign, but a father should be for ever. You will need to meet him first, Nathaniel, and understand what it is you offer.'

'Then let me, Sandrine. Let me get to know both of you again in a way we did not have the chance of before. In fact, let us begin right now. I can tell you something of my life as a child and then you can tell me yours.'

Her smile was tentative.

'After my parents died my grandfather found it hard to cope. He left me in the hands of a nanny and myriad servants and went to Italy for three years. When he returned home I was sent straight up to Eton. From the age of nine to the age of eighteen I barely saw him. When I did I found he was a man I couldn't like and I am sure that the feeling is mutual.'

'Where is he now?'

'At St Auburn. He rarely leaves the place and I seldom go there. Such an arrangement works for us both.'

'You never had sisters or brothers?'

'No. My mother had a difficult birth with me and could not have other babies. Perhaps that was a part of my grandfather's dislike.'

'Surely a grown man could not blame a small child for such a thing.'

His smile widened. 'My point exactly.'

With the wind in his hair and the sun on his face Nathaniel Lindsay looked to Cassandra like the epitome of a wealthy and favoured lord of the peerage. He also looked maddeningly beautiful, a fact that worried her even more than the détente that they spoke of.

She wondered if she could withstand such a thing and not give in to the feelings that swirled inside her. This time she was no *ingénue* with a hard-luck story as the unfortunate victim of crime. No, now she was the one who had betrayed honour and had the scars to prove it. With only the shedding of clothes would he see the living, breathing marks of treason branded into her right breast.

Hence she moved away. From touch. From closeness. From temptation. His confession about his relationship with his grandfather was worth more to her than all the gold and riches in the world because for the first time she saw the child who had made the man.

'I don't know what it would be like to be an only child. Through all the years of our early childhood it was my siblings' presence that made everything seem bearable.'

'You think that Jamie needs a brother or a sister?'

Despite meaning not to she laughed. 'A gentleman should not mention such a thing, Lord Lindsay.'

The dimple in his right cheek was deep and

whilst he was speaking so candidly of his past she did not wish to waste the chance of knowledge. 'What is St Auburn like?'

'The house was built in the sixteenth century by a Lindsay ancestor and has been added on to ever since. It sits in the midst of rolling farmland and there is a lake it looks down upon.'

'It sounds like a home that needs to be filled with family and laughter.'

Nathaniel smiled. 'Perhaps you are right. Are you always so wise, Cassandra Northrup?'

'If I was, I doubt I would have needed to go to France in the first place. I might have recovered from my mother's death like a normal child and been a proper lady of society with all the airs and graces.'

'I like you better as you are.'

The blush began as a small warm spot near her heart and spread to the corners of her body. Out in the air in the quiet winds of late summer it was so easy to believe in such troth.

'You do not really know me at all, Nathaniel.'

'Then let me. Come to St Auburn. Bring Maureen and Kenyon Riley. Bring whomever you like to feel comfortable, and come with Jamie.'

The grey in his eyes was fathomless today, a lover who would show her only what he might think she wished to see. He was good at hiding things, she thought, the trait of a spy imposed upon everyday life. She wondered how easy that would be, to live with secrets that could result in the downfall of governments if told. Her own had been a hard enough task to keep hidden.

When a group of well-dressed ladies accompanied by their maids walked into the park they were forced to return to the road, though once there awkwardness enveloped her. On the street she saw others watching him, a well-known lord with the promise of an earldom as a mantle around his shoulders. With Nathaniel Lindsay she could not afford to make a mistake or go too lightly into the promises that he asked of her.

Jamie's welfare rested on good decisions and proper judgement. No, she would rest on his suggestions for a while until she had mulled them over.

An hour later, Nathaniel sat in his leather chair behind the large mahogany desk in his study and looked about the room without really seeing anything.

He had a son. Jamie. James Nathanael Colbert Northrup, she had said, his name sandwiched in between her own.

He should have asked Cassandra other things, should have found out what Jamie liked and what he didn't. Did he read, did he love horses, did he play with balls, did he have a pet?

Almost four years old. For a man with little contact with children the number was difficult to get his head around. What could a nearly four-year-old boy do? Sitting back against the seat, he closed his eyes.

God, he was a father. He was a father to a child conceived in the wilds of the Pyrenees above Perpignan.

He took a silver flask from the drawer and unstopped it. Cassandra had been on edge, the usual flare of awareness between them doused by responsibility and worry. Did she think he might take their son away or insist upon the legality of their marriage?

Legality.

The child was a legitimate heir to the St Auburn earldom and fortune. Nat wondered just what his grandfather, William Harper Wilson Lindsay, would say to that.

The past few days had been full of surprises. Yesterday in Wallingford he had discovered another girl had been murdered in the exact same way as those in London. He also had the name of the tall and well-dressed Londoner who had left his room at the inn the day the body had been discovered.

Scrivener Weeks.

Nat had spent a good few hours since last night trawling through the names of all those in society, but come up with nothing.

His mind reeled with all that had happened and as he took a sip of his brandy he smiled.

Chapter Eleven

Jamie was sick, the temperature he ran more worrying by the hour, and Cassandra was increasingly beginning to panic, something she seldom did in any medical emergency.

Her mind would not be still as she imagined all the possibilities and problems that could befall her son if the fever didn't begin to abate. Maureen had helped her with the nursing for most of the day, but had gone now with Kenyon Riley to a dinner with the old duke in Belgravia. His nanny, Mrs Harris, had also been here for the past hours, but Cassie could see that she was tired and so sent her off to bed.

Hence she was alone, the weak and pain-filled moans cutting through all sense and making her as fearful as she had ever been. By eleven o'clock she had had enough. Scrawling out a note, she asked for one of the Northrup servants to deliver it immediately to the Lindsay town house and wait for an answer.

She wanted Nathaniel here. She wanted a man who might love her son as much as she did and who could bring some sense and calm into a situation that was spiralling out of control for her. A tiny whisper that predicted Jamie might not recover was also part of the reason. If her son died, then Nathaniel would never have seen him. She shook the thought away and ordered back sanity.

It was a simple fever with a high and sudden temperature probably brought on by the dousing he had had in a rain shower in the garden. Visions of young children who went on to develop rashes and stiff necks came too, however, and she had seen enough of life in the past years to know that things did not always turn out happily.

Yesterday in the park Nathaniel had offered her the chance of reconciliation. Tonight all she wanted was his strength and his composure. She tried to regulate her breathing so that Jamie would not pick up on her panic, but found that the beat of her heart was going faster and faster, a clammy dread beginning to take over completely.

She should have called the doctor, she knew she should have, but the Northrup physician was a man who still believed in doing things in his way and even after she had stressed a number of times to him the importance of clean hands and tools he had not taken up the learning. Her father had wanted to replace him, but the traditions of the Batemans attending the Cowper family in the capacity of medical practitioners had been a difficult one to break and so he had given up. Usually Cassandra dealt with any sickness and she did it with such acumen and success they seldom asked for the physician's attendance.

Jamie was so deathly still, that was the problem, and the lukewarm water that she sponged his little body with was making no inroads to a gathering heat. She had used infusions of camphor, basil and lemon balm, angelica and hyssop, yet nothing seemed to be making any difference.

The sound of footsteps had her standing, heart in mouth, and she turned to the door as Nathaniel walked through, his shirt opened at the collar as if he had not even had the time to find a necktie, pale eyes taking in the scene before him without any sign of panic.

Cassie burst into tears, an action so unexpected and unfamiliar that she even surprised herself for having done so. He did not break a step as he gathered her into his arms and brought her with him over to the bed, his eyes hungrily taking in the features of his son.

'How long has Jamie had the fever?'

'All…day.' She swallowed, trying to make her voice sound more like it usually did.

'You have bathed him?'

'Many times, and I have used up all my remedies.'

Jamie's fit began with a twitch and a quiver, the right side of his body tensing and moving in a rigidity that spread to his legs and feet. While paralysing fear held Cassandra immobile, Nathaniel whipped off the thin sheet and spread it on the floor, lifting Jamie down to lie on his side and crouching by him.

He did not restrain him or hold him in any way, but let the shaking take its course for ten seconds and then twenty, just watching to make sure that he did not injure himself with the movement. Finally, when Cassandra thought it might never pass, Jamie relaxed, vomiting across the boots of his father.

'So this is what it is to be a parent?' Nathaniel turned towards her, his hand passing across the forehead of his son and relief evident.

Nodding, she thought that she had never loved Nathaniel more than she did at that moment, his certainty and strength edged with gentle compassion and humour.

'I had the same sort of fits when I was a child, Cassandra, and the St Auburn physician assured my mother and father that they would disappear as I grew older. Which they did. He will be fine. Better than my boots, at least.'

He leaned over to wipe the traces of moisture from his fine dark-brown Hessians, the gleam of leather a little tarnished. 'If you straighten the bed, I will lift him back up for I think the worst is over now.'

Nathaniel felt as though he were lifting treasure, his son, the small and damp body smelling of sickness and fatigue. Yet he was beautiful in the way only small boys could be, a scrape upon his left kneecap as if he had been running somewhere too fast and his colouring exactly that of a St Auburn heritage.

The same dark hair and skin tone, the same line of nose and cheek he had seen in the drawings of himself as a child. His heart turned in his chest and squeezed with a feeling that was foreign, half fear and all love, the utter storm of fatherhood beaching upon him, winding him with its intensity, fervour and suddenness.

'Thank you for calling me.'

'Thank you for coming.'

'He is beautiful.'

'I think so.' For a second a smile tweaked at the corner of her lips, the worry and fright beaten back a little, the tears drying on her cheeks.

'Is it the first time this has happened?'

'It is. Jamie is usually so well and full of energy. It was the fright of the difference, I think.'

'I had three of these fits across the space of a year when I was about his age and, according to my mother's diary, she was always as worried as you appear to be.'

Jamie suddenly opened his eyes, the pale grey confused. 'Mama?'

'I am here, darling.' Cassandra took his hand and brought it to her lips, kissing the fingers one by one. 'You have been sick, but you are getting better now.' The small face came around, questions contained within it.

'This is Nathaniel Colbert Lindsay, Jamie.'

'Nearly my name?'

'He is your—'

'Papa.' Jamie finished the sentence, and that one word sealed a lifetime of loyalty. Glancing over, Nathaniel saw Cassandra nod, and he came down on his knees beside the bed to take the offered hand of his son. Warm fingers curled into his.

For ever.

'I used to get sick like this when I was little, so I know exactly what to do and you will soon feel a lot better.'

'Did you come from France?'

'Pardon?' Was confusion a part of this sickness?

'No, Jamie. Your papa lives in London now so you may see him when you want to.'

'Can you stay here now?'

'Can I?' Nat looked over at Cassandra and smiled when she nodded. 'It seems that I can.'

'Good.' With that Jamie simply closed his eyes and went to sleep, his breathing even and the fever that had ravaged his body less than a few moments past, broken.

The silence stretched around them all, the gratitude of seeing a small child's recovery being a big part of that. His wife clasped Jamie's hand on one side of the bed and he held the other, a link of family and vigilance and concern. Outside distant bells chimed the hour of twelve, as the night softened into quiet.

'Would you like a cup of tea? I could go down to the kitchens and make it and then bring it back here.'

Tea? Nat would have far rather had a stiff brandy, but he wondered how she might feel about drinking in a child's room so he nodded at the offered drink. He felt as if he had been plunged into a different world where everything was altered and extraordinary. But right somehow. He smiled at that fact.

Left alone with his son, Nathaniel observed every feature, every part of a child who had been conceived out of love. He was sleeping now, his lashes dark against his cheeks and one arm curled beneath his head. He had slept like that, too, as a child, he remembered, and smiled as he noticed a ragged teddy bear on the floor, a well-loved companion by the looks of it. Picking it up, he tucked it beside his son.

Just another one of all the small moments of a childhood he had missed, he thought, and resolved not to lose more.

When Cassandra bustled back a few moments later with a tray in hand she gestured to him to follow her into a sitting room close by and then proceeded to set out the cups, sugar and milk on a table.

'I thought if we had our tea here it would not disturb Jamie and yet we are still near enough to hear if he calls out.' She tipped her head to listen, but no noise was forthcoming. 'His nanny and the servants are all in their beds and I did not wish to wake them again so if you need something to eat…?'

'Just tea would be lovely.'

A flash of humour answered him as she understood his meaning. 'Papa does not drink at all and so our house isn't well stocked with liquor. But I will make certain that some is brought in for you next time.'

'Next time?'

'Jamie wants you in his life. Even being so sick he told you he did.'

'And what of you? Do you want me here?'

She lifted her cup carefully and looked at him directly. 'I do.'

'Then let us begin with that.'

The tea tasted like an elixir the way she made it with a dollop of milk and sugar. It was steadying after a night of emotion. He wondered why he had never taken to the brew before and resolved to instruct his staff to get this particular leaf into his house for drinking. Everything seemed heightened somehow: the scent of Cassandra's perfume, the colour of her hair. The small touch of her skin against his thumb as she had handed him the cup and the earthy aroma of tea.

Tonight lust did not rule as it usually did when they met, although in truth it simmered beneath the conversation. No, this evening a shared responsibility had engendered new emotions. Contentment. Peace. Gratitude. The quieter humours that Nat had seldom experienced before. The joy of sitting in a room with family around him and being a part of a tradition that stretched back through the ages.

'I could buy him a horse, a small one with a good temperament. One that did not kick. A safe steed.'

She smiled. 'You cannot protect him from everything, Nathaniel. What was your first horse like?'

'Wild. A real hellion. I learnt almost immediately where to stand and where not to.'

'The lessons of life. These are what Jamie needs to know from you.'

'Is it always this hard? Being a parent, I mean.'

'From the very first moment when the midwife handed him to me my heart ceased to be my own.'

'You had others there with you?'

'No.'

He swore softly so that the sound of it would not inadvertently reach the ears of his son. 'I wish I had been present.'

'I did, too, but I thought you were dead. I looked for you in Paris and asked after you. No one had ever heard your name, of course, and you were probably already back in England. But I did not know any of that then.'

'When you came to London you did not arrive as Mrs Colbert?'

'I thought it too dangerous. I had no idea as to what had happened to Guy Lebansart and his men and I wanted to keep Jamie as safely away from them as I could. I thought placing your name within his would be enough for you to know what had happened if anything should go wrong with me and you were still alive to find him.'

'And you were condemned for not using the name of your husband because of it?'

'Oh, that was an easy sufferance for I seldom strayed into society and finally the gossip lessened.'

'If you had used Colbert I might have found you earlier.'

'Then that would be my only regret.'

'Come with me to St Auburn when Jamie is better. I can show you both the beauty of it, the solidness.'

'You said your grandfather was there.'

'Come as my family and he can meet you.'

Nathaniel wanted Jamie and her to go to St Auburn. He wanted things that she could not promise just yet with the scars at her breast and the guilt in her heart.

Tonight it had been easy to pretend with Jamie between them. Tonight he had come like a knight in shining armour through the darkness to rescue her. But tomorrow...?

Reality would creep back with the anger and then she would be at the mercy of pity again. She needed to make sure that the feelings in

France could be translated here away from any pressures before she followed him into a place that neither of them could come back from. She needed him to love her wholly with his body just as he had done once in the southern mountains and she wanted to love him back in the same way. But could she risk asking that of him? Now, after Jamie's sickness and the care he had shown, would the scars ruin everything?

The thrall of memory took her breath away. 'Do you live alone at your town house?'

'Yes.' His voice was quiet, underlaced with question.

'Then perhaps I could come there first. Just me…'

She left the rest unsaid, but he had picked up on the implications instantly.

'When?'

'Tomorrow night. At eight.' That gave her a day to make certain that Jamie was fully re-covered.

'I would like that.'

'And it will only be us?'

'Yes.'

'I will need a carriage later…to bring me home before the morning.'

'It shall be at your disposal.'

*'I am half sick of shadows,' said The
Lady of Shalott.*

Cassie just hoped that by leaving her sanctuary and following her heart into the arms of
her Lancelot the result would be much happier
than the one in the poem.

*Out flew the web and floated wide;
The mirror crack'd from side to side;
'The curse is come upon me,' cried
The Lady of Shalott.*

The three scars from Lebansart's blade
burnt like hot ribbons of shame upon her
breast.

After such a night Nathaniel was unable to
sleep and so he sat at the desk in his office and
worked on the case of the girls found near the
river. Rearranging scraps of paper before him,
he took away this one and replaced with that.

The list contained the names of every member of the Venus Club. The clues had to be
here somewhere, he knew, the intuition that

had served him so well in his years of working with the Service honed and on high alert.

Scrivener Weeks would be here somewhere hiding amongst the detail, he just had to find out where he was concealed. Removing each member who was neither tall nor dark, he was left with the names of fifteen men. Reginald Northrup's name caught his attention, but so did the name of Christopher Hanley.

Another thought occurred. It was Hanley who had told the world that he had seen Cassandra in the environs of Whitechapel Road and Hanley who had been disparaging about the role of the Daughters of the Poor trying to save every wayward girl in London. Could the existence of Cassandra's charity be threatening him in some way; threatening his preference for sexual experiences with very young women?

Placing the name in the very centre of all the others, Nat determined to find out more about his family circumstances and his night-time habits. He would visit Hanley, too. Sometimes it just took a more direct approach to flush out a guilty quarry and make them run.

Meanwhile, he would make absolutely certain that Cassandra came nowhere near the vicinity of her uncle's friend.

Chapter Twelve

Cassie could barely settle to anything for the whole of the next day, a sort of wild excitement that verged on panic underlying everything she did.

Jamie was so much better, leaving his bed and eating large plates of whatever the cook tempted him with. Maureen was astonished at how much improved he seemed, though it was another matter entirely that she quizzed Cassandra about.

'There is word you had a visitor late last night, Cassie. Lord Nathaniel Lindsay was an unexpected caller?'

Cassandra knew her sister's ways. Maureen obviously had found out a lot more about the unusual happening and was waiting for Cassandra to unravel it for her.

'Lord Lindsay looks familiar somehow. I cannot quite put my finger on how I should know him, but…?'

At that precise moment Jamie ran past playing with a small train, and it was if a shutter had suddenly been raised.

'Oh, my goodness, Lindsay is Jamie's father? Nathanael is his second name?'

Horror stood where a humorous playfulness had lingered a moment before. 'He ruined you?'

'No. We were married, Reena. In France, almost five years ago. Everything is perfectly legal.'

'Then why…?' She could not even formulate her next question.

'One day I will tell you everything, but not at this moment. If you could keep my confidence for a little while longer, I would be most appreciative.'

'He will not break your heart again?'

'Again?' She could not quite understand what her sister alluded to.

'You came home from Paris like a half person and never looked at another male with any thoughts of interest although there were many good men who were offering. I knew there was someone. I just thought he was dead.'

There are worse ways to be separated than in death, Cassie thought as Jamie came over to her to demand a cuddle. Her sister's dark eyes watched carefully.

'Kenyon likes him. I do, too.'

'Who does he like?' Jamie's voice put paid to any further conversation.

In the late afternoon Cassie fussed about which gown to put on and finally decided on a dark yellow silk, a little outdated but beautifully cut. She fashioned her own hair into a bun at her nape, decorating the sides with two ornate tortoiseshell combs she had procured in the Marais. Cassie reasoned that if the night was to play out as she hoped she needed a style that would be easily unpinned and quickly redone when she left in the early hours of the next day.

Even the thought of it all made her apprehensive. Such a premeditated and deliberate choice. The hands of the clock seemed to race towards eight, and her stomach felt agitated and jittery.

She was twenty-three and she had had just

one lover for only a short time. She did not count the Baudoins' rough handling of her in the first days of Nay, preferring to forget about the violence and hurt of the place. No, all she remembered now were the weeks between Saint Estelle and Perpignan, and the utter need they had felt for each other, the desire and the passion.

Breathing, she held in her hope as an aching desperateness. Could this happen again or had she ruined it with her choice of sacrificing others so that they might live?

She turned to the mirror and looked at herself. She was not a bad person or a deceitful one. She had done her best ever since the betrayal at Perpignan to make amends for the harm that she had caused. Would Nathaniel see that of her? Would he be able to look beyond the past and see a future?

'Please, God, let it be so,' she whispered and hurried to find shoes, stockings and a coat to match her gown.

Cassandra arrived on the dot of eight-fifteen, the ornate clock in the corner of the front entrance still calling out the quarter-hour. She had come. Dismissing his man, Nat went out to the carriage to open the door, the large black cape she wore hiding much, though her eyes shone through in the dark, anxious and fearful.

'Is Jamie better today?' A topic other than this want that hung between them was welcomed, and she smiled.

'He is, my lord.' She allowed the Lindsay servant to take her cloak.

'So formal, my lady.'

At that she blushed heavily, and would have tripped on the hem of her yellow gown had he not placed his hand beneath her arm. God, all he wanted to do was to snatch her up and take her to his bed, to assuage a pummelling need that was gaining more traction with every single second.

Friendship.

The word came back, loud with inherent meaning. He needed to slow down and calm down, for Cassandra Northrup deserved so much more than a quick tumble of lust, devoid of chivalry and consideration.

'Dinner is waiting in the dining room. After that I shall dismiss the servants and...' He did not finish.

'A meal sounds lovely.' She smiled at him

then, as though she understood in his unfinished sentence some shared disquiet.

'The French chef from St Auburn followed me down to London and is very competent. I hope you will enjoy the fare.' Lord, why was he rambling on like this? He sounded like a green youth in the first throes of pleasing a girl, so he bit down for silence. He hardly recognised himself in his concern for making the right impression.

When he had visited Hawk earlier in the afternoon to tell him his worries about Hanley he had also mentioned the proposed dinner with Cassandra Northrup. With all good intentions Stephen had instructed him to smile a lot and be most attentive, but for the life of him Nat couldn't seem to make his lips curl upwards and empty compliments had never been his style.

Instead, he pulled the chair from the table and invited Cassandra to sit and then he took his own place a good few feet away. Distance made him less edgy and the procession of kitchen staff with tureens of soup and entrées turned his mind for a moment from the reason as to why she was here alone tonight.

'I don't think I thanked you properly for

your help with Jamie the other night, Nathaniel. I do not normally panic.'

'I was glad that you called me, and if he is anything like me and has another fit it should be months away.'

'You only had three episodes, you said.'

'Indeed. I outgrew them exactly as the St Auburn physician had predicted that I would.'

'A family trait, then?'

'My father was prone to the same as a child. He did not have brothers or sisters, however, so I am not certain if it would have been something that ran through the whole line.'

'Well, it is reassuring to know that you recovered.' She drew a spoon of soup to her mouth and sighed. 'Onion soup. This is a taste I remember, though I have not had it since Paris.'

'You did not think to send word to your father after Perpignan and ask him to help?'

She shook her head, the red-gold catching the light from the chandelier above in a sparkling cascade of colour. 'Papa would have found the situation trying, and as a family we attempt to shelter him from anything that is difficult. After Mama died he was…brittle and I am not certain if he will ever be truly happy again.'

'So you managed alone?'

'I did.'

'You do that often.'

Her spoon hovered above the plate. 'I believe in myself more now.'

'I am glad for it.'

'I believe that atonement goes a certain way in alleviating past mistakes, and that what was, is not always the same as what will be.'

'Wise of you.'

'I have made errors, Nathaniel, big ones that I wish every single day I had not, but in the end one cannot wish life away. One has to confront it with courage and go on.'

'And you have.'

She nodded. 'For Jamie's sake, I had to.'

The strength of her washed across him. She sat there and told him that in adversity she had found a version of herself that she liked. He wanted to reach over and bring her ruined hand to his lips and kiss each finger one by one. She was no empty-headed maiden trying to fit in with others' perceptions of her and whereas Acacia had been hardened by the problems in her life, Cassandra had been freed by them.

He wished he had skipped the course of soup and gone instead for more simple fare because the hours were running away with the task of eating and there was still dessert. He was glad the removes of soup had been taken away and hoped the offering of lobster, ham and venison might disappear just as quickly. He could not remember a meal taking quite as long as he helped himself perfunctorily to one of the many plates of vegetables.

Cassandra felt hot and uneasy. The food was beautifully cooked and expensive and yet she could barely eat it. A clock in the house kept striking out the minutes of every hour and time seemed to be racing towards the real reason as to why she was here.

She wanted to sleep with Nathaniel Lindsay, she did. She wanted to feel him inside her moving with the passion only he could engender and she longed for the quiet repose of skin against skin, their bodies speaking in a way words never did.

But the scars of Lebansart were a reminder of all that had gone wrong between them and she dreaded him seeing them and asking about what had happened. She breathed out heavily and knew that he watched her with his beautiful pale-grey eyes, the dimple in his right cheek seen under the bright candelabras.

She would not survive again if he turned her away. For all her bravado and independence she understood that. The lobster felt dry in her mouth as she tried to swallow it, helping herself to a generous sip of white wine with the taste of summer in its bouquet. She seldom drank anything stronger than tea, save for in his company, where fortitude was as necessary as breath.

Cassie wished the meal would end and that the servants might disappear. She wanted him to lead her to his chamber with the minimum of chatter and undress her with the maximum of speed. She wanted to look into his eyes when he saw the scars and see acceptance or indifference, it did not matter which. It was the bewildering bloom of distaste that she hoped so fervently to avoid.

He suddenly stood. 'Perhaps we might leave the rest for later, Cassandra.' Those attending to the table stepped back and waited while he helped her from her seat.

As they reached the hall leading to the stairwell he petitioned her to tarry for a moment whilst he returned to give his instructions to the staff. She could hear his voice asking them to clean up and then retire for he would not be requiring their services further this evening. The resulting silence was full of question and speculation, but even that did not worry Cassie.

Then he was back again, taking her hand and escorting her up the wide marble staircase into the second floor of the house. His room lay at the end of a corridor, a set of French doors with an ornate gold handle and a substantial lock. As she walked through she heard him turn the key. Privacy. She was thankful for it.

His chamber was decorated in all shades of pale, a restful luxurious interior that threw her off balance. The heavy brocades of paisley and floral at the Northrup town house looked tacky and overdone in comparison. This room was one of bleached furniture and patinas harking back to the age of a faded beauty. She wondered if he had had a hand in choosing the decor.

A whole line of leatherbound books sat on the table beside the bed. When he saw where she looked he commented, 'I read a lot.'

She remembered he had told her of that once and she had wondered. No amount of guessing could have placed him as a cultured English lord, however, with the lineage of an old family on his shoulders and a library of books at his disposal.

'You keep surprising me,' she managed to say.

At that he laughed, loudly, the first truly free emotion of the evening. A frisson of need made her stiffen. 'I could say the same, Cassandra. Few people manage to keep me as intrigued as you do and so effortlessly.'

He had come closer now. If she stepped forward she could have rested her head against his heart. With all her willpower she stopped herself doing just that.

Not yet, a voice inside her called. *He needs to understand exactly who you are.*

Her fingers came up to loosen the ties at her bodice. They were shaking in their pursuit of truth as fire began to build behind the slate of his eyes. The yellow silk had been chosen carefully. With just a few twitches of fabric it fell from her shoulders, the thin bodice of lawn the only thing now that kept his glance from her shame.

Then that was gone, too, three slices of

raised red skin at the top of her right breast on show.

'I did not give the names as easily as you had imagined, Nathaniel. I paid for their lives in my own blood, too. I knew that I was pregnant, you see, and if I did not give him something he might...'

'God.' One finger reached out to trace the injuries, horror and anger on his face.

But not at her. It was Lebansart his wrath was directed at.

'The bastard did this to you?'

She nodded because suddenly she could not speak, the back of her throat closing in an aching heaviness.

'He could have killed you. Both of you.'

'I th-think he thought he had.'

'Ah, sweetheart.' His voice broke as he simply leant down and kissed the scars, one by one. Healing their ugliness, she was to think later, and dissipating their power over her. Forgiveness was a quiet and gentle emotion, the light and earnest feel of his tongue and the smooth sweep of his lips, but it held all the weight of a new beginning.

Her hand came through his hair, shorter now

than it had been in France, the dark sheen of it almost blue.

'Love me, Nathaniel, and make me forget.'

In response he lifted her to him and brought her to his bed, the wide velvet counterpane beneath her as he peeled the dress and bodice away. Her stockings were next and the small slippers bought only a few days before. Then he loosened her hair from its tie and draped the length of it down beside her.

Caught in the light and in his gaze she stayed very still. 'You are even more beautiful than I remember.' His voice held reverence and awe.

He was fully dressed as he stroked one breast, smiling when the nipple puckered at his ministrations. Then his fingers fell lower, across her stomach and down into the place between her thighs, pushing into the wet warmth with a gentle insistence. And all the time his eyes never left her own, the fire within them banking and a look that said she was his. Need made her loins rise from the bed to meet him, her legs opening wider to allow him in, and she looked away because she knew that the roiling waves of release were about to come and she did not want to see his reaction to such a surrender.

Her muscles caught around his fingers, stilling the plunder and keeping him there inside her tight, and when she began to shake he pushed in farther still, eliciting a groan that held a primal relief.

She was no longer cautious or circumspect. All she could think of was the aching craving urgency in her body and the balm and ease of tension.

They belonged together, Nathaniel and she, and it had nothing to do with marriage or legality or expectations.

It was far simpler than that. It was how their skin called to each other and how the shape of his body so perfectly fitted hers. It was in the scent of him and the beauty and the strength. It was in his honesty and morality and bravery and forgiveness.

A single tear traced its way from her left eye down onto the pillow beneath. She had not expected absolution, but how she had wanted it. From him. From the only other person in all of the world who might understand what she had lost and what she had gained.

Her saviour. Now and then.

'I will love you for ever, Nathaniel.'

* * *

Cassandra's eyes were clear and her voice was strong as she said it, no half-meant troth given with a lack of honesty or intent.

'For ever?'

This time he was ready and there was no question in his reply. With care he crossed the room and opened a drawer, pulling out his mother's ring from a velvet box. The emerald glinted in the light as he walked back and he saw she was now perched on the edge of his bed, watching.

With care he bent on one knee and the smile that he had missed so much came easily to her lips.

'I never stopped loving you, Cassandra Northrup. Will you marry me?'

'I already have, Nathaniel Lindsay.' The words were wobbly and tears pooled in her eyes.

'Again then. Properly this time. With everyone around us.'

'Yes.'

Bringing her hand up, he placed the ring upon it. His mother's ring was still oversized and the ancient gold needed a good polish, but on Cassandra's finger it looked completely right.

A circle. Of life. Lost and found. He knew his mother would have loved Cassandra, loved her rarity and her honesty. The only thing she wore was a smile and this ring and she looked to him like a goddess sent from above. To heal loneliness and doubt, to bring laughter and adventure and truth.

When her hands came to the buttons on his shirt he stood still, tugging the garment off on completion and then doing the same with his trousers and boots. Life had marked them both. Inside and out. But it had also melded them together into a shape that could not withstand the world alone. He smote the candles above and the one on the stand near the bed and in the light of the fire he turned. They came together as husband and wife, his seed spilled without a care for caution.

Home. Safe. The night outside and the warmth within.

'I want as many more Jamies as you might give me,' he whispered finally when sense had returned.

'Starting tonight, Nathaniel.' The light in her eyes danced as her fingers closed around his shaft and all that had been wonderful before began again.

* * *

Much later they spoke. She leaned against him, her head upon his chest as he lifted himself to sit against the cushioned bed end.

'Lebansart left the minute after I gave him the names on the document. Louis Baudoin had already died from having allowed me to see the paper and in the end it killed Celeste, too...'

His finger came across her lips, stopping the flow of words. 'You don't have to tell me any more if you do not wish to. It doesn't matter now.'

'But I want to. If I had not interfered, my cousin's soul may have been saved, for she died by her own hand less than a day later.'

'Guilt has as many lives as you wish to give it, Cassandra. You were young and trying to do your best to save those you loved, but it's time now to stop the blame.'

'I hated her sometimes,' she whispered, the very words so dreadful she could not give them the full power of sound.

'Celeste?'

'She made me stay there with her. I could have escaped, but she held me there with her weakness and her need. In the end she understood just how foolish she had been, but for a long while she revelled in it. The wine. Louis Baudoin. The danger. I could never trust that she would not be harmed by her lack of foresight and so I stayed.'

'To protect her?'

She nodded, the brisk anger in the movement revealing. 'And finally I could not even do that.'

'Voltaire once wrote that "no snowflake in an avalanche ever feels responsible". Perhaps you should allow your cousin more of the burden of blame.'

Cassandra mulled his words over. Celeste had grown up reprimanding everyone except herself when things went wrong and in every situation had put her own needs first.

'You think each person is accountable for their actions.'

'I do. I am the next in line for the St Auburn title and all it entails, yet the duties that came with my job in Europe were never the ones my grandfather wished for me to entertain. It was his way of life or no way of life and he harboured a resentment I could never understand.'

'Sometimes people disappoint you.'

He laughed. 'I try to allow them not to.'

Lifting her head on to her hands, she looked at him. 'Did your work in France teach you the knack of knowing what it is that others wish to hear?'

He frowned. 'Hawk and Lucas helped me more with that. You have not met Luc Clairmont yet for he is in the Americas, but without them I wouldn't have survived the loneliness of my childhood.'

She ran her finger across his chest, circling the skin around his nipple and liking the way it tightened. 'I often worried that someone might come from England and arrest me after Perpignan, and in my dreams the punishment was always death. Perhaps that was a part of the reason I didn't come home for so long. You worked for the British Service, but you never told anyone about me.'

His hand clamped down across hers. 'I couldn't. I never asked another question of that time because if I had found out you were dead….'

'You kept me safe. Us safe.'

'Then I am glad. But enough of talk, my beautiful wife, for there are still some hours before we need to rise.'

When he rolled her beneath him she simply relaxed, opening her mouth as his lips came across her own.

He heard the birdsong at dawn but remained perfectly still. Cassandra lay against him, one leg draped across his thigh and her head tucked into the crook of his arm. Her hair cascaded around them in all the shades of gold and red, wildly tangled and curling. He lifted up one tress and felt its softness.

His wife. They had slept for much longer than she could have wanted to and for that he was pleased.

No covert sneaking back home. He did not wish for only night-time trysts. He wanted to see the sunshine play across her skin and know the ecstasy of every hour of the day in bed. Not quite the slow-building friendship she had had in mind, but then nothing about their relationship had ever been ordinary. He wondered how she might explain this night away to her family.

Her breathing changed and her eyes opened, sleep filled and disorientated, but widening as they recognised daylight at the window. Yet still she made no attempt to leave.

'You kept me up too late, sir,' she whispered, and there was a smile in her rebuke.

'Can I do so again tonight, Lady Lindsay? Or today if you should so will it?'

'I cannot think your servants would be pleased at such a prospect.' Lifting her head, she listened for a moment. 'They are at work already, yet they have not come in?'

'And rest assured that they will not, my love.'

Her left hand pushed back the heavy length of her hair and the ring of his mother glinted in the light.

'However, the grapevines of those in servitude will be ringing and my name, undoubtedly, shall be bandied around the salons in shock.'

'I'll announce our wish to marry in *The Times* tomorrow and everyone in the *ton* will recognise you as my intended. No one then would dare to criticise.'

'And your grandfather?'

'Who knows? Such a pronouncement may even bring him from St Auburn as he has hoped for such an occasion for ever. Jamie's existence will make him delirious.'

'You almost make me believe that it could be this easy for us.'

'Well, we have waited for years to be together again and that must be some kind of a miracle.'

She curled into him, holding tight. 'I have missed you. Missed this. Missed talking and loving. Missed closeness.'

He felt her breath at his throat, gentle and honest. Like his life was now with her in it. He wanted to protect her for ever and love her until they were old and grey with a million memories shared between them. The harsh and raw realities of the past faded into this new serenity, Cassandra and Jamie in the very centre of a world reformed.

Her finger traced the tattoo on his forearm. 'What does this mean?'

He smiled. 'It's one of the symbols from the healing temples of Asclepius. At the time, in the backstreets of Marseilles, I was looking for resurrection and renewal. Later on it always reminded me of the thin line between life and death.'

'Being a spy must have been dangerous work. Your body is covered in scars.'

'It's the price one pays for not carrying arms

and being out of uniform. Blending into a community is not always as easy as it might sound.'

'But you have stopped?'

'Almost.'

'I am glad for it.'

'And for the first time I think I could settle at St Auburn and run the place, farm the land, sit as a judge at the country courts, grow vegetables. All the things I once would not have seen sense in.'

She laughed.

'With you and Jamie there it all feels possible.'

Cassie turned then to look at him, the light in her eyes bright and clear. He could never decide whether they were more green than blue. Today they seemed an exact mixture of both. 'I think I loved you the first moment I saw you in Nay, with your dimple…here.' She touched his cheek.

'Show me,' he returned and brought her against him, the sunlight from the new day creating a river of warmth on their bed.

They renewed their vows two days later in the chapel to one side of the Lindsay town house and it was a small and private occasion. Stephen Hawkhurst was the best man and Maureen the bridesmaid. William Lindsay, the old Earl of St Auburn, had sent a note declining his attendance. Cassandra's sister Anne had not been able to make the journey down from her home in Scotland because she was expecting her fourth child.

'You look beautiful, Cassandra,' Nathaniel said as she came down the stairs, her gown of cream silk shimmering in the new day.

'The seamstress you organised was wonderfully fast and this time around I even have shoes.'

He laughed and took her hand, but poignancy lingered beneath the humour as both thought of the small house by the river.

'Now and for ever,' he whispered, brushing his lips across her cheek despite the onlookers, and Jamie standing between them wriggled in delight.

When the clergyman called them to an altar fashioned with flowers, the three of them linked hands and walked forward, her father, brother and Kenyon Riley just behind them.

'Dearly beloved, we have come together in the presence of God to witness and bless the

joining together of this man and this woman
in holy matrimony...'

They looked at each other. This time they
would be married under their own names,
properly formed and completely legal.

A few hours later Stephen asked if he might
speak to them both in the library where they
would not be disturbed. After shutting the door
he brought forth a leather satchel and took out
a wad of documents from within.

'I have a wedding present for you both.'

Nat stepped forward, the frown on his brow
giving Cassie the inkling that he might know
what was held within the papers. They looked
important. Her own heart began to beat fast.

'It is the official report from the British Service about the events that transpired in Perpignan after you were hurt in Languedoc, Nat.'

'God.' Her husband's curse was soft.

'It is not what you might think,' Hawk said
quickly and handed him over the account. 'I
have underlined the most crucial parts. Perhaps
your wife might like to hear them.'

'No.' Her own voice, stiff with shock. How
could Stephen Hawkhurst do this to her? She
knew what would be within the letter, knew it

to the bottom of her breaking heart. But Nathaniel was smiling and there was the suspicion of tears in his eyes as he began to read.

So it is concluded that on the fifth of November 1846 at about nine p.m. two masked men broke into the house of Mr Didier Desrosiers and Mr Gilbert Desrosiers in Toulouse, France, and killed each of them with two shots to the head.

Our agent in Languedoc, Nathaniel Lindsay, was also found on the right bank of the Basse River in Perpignan in the afternoon of the sixth of November 1846 with injuries to his head, stomach and right arm received by unknown enemies of England.

Despite extensive searching the perpetrators have never been brought to justice.

The fifth of November? The day before they had reached Perpignan. The day before she had told Lebansart the names. The day before she had branded herself a traitor. The day before shame had been scorched into memory.

'It was not me, after all.' The words slipped

from her, tentative and unbelieving. 'They were already dead?'

'How did you know to find this?' Nat spoke now directly to Stephen, the relief in his tone evident.

'When you said you had married Cassandra Northrup in France I knew that you would not have done such a thing lightly. When you then went on to say that she had betrayed you, I realised there must be more to the affair than you had told me. At the Forsythe ball your wife made it known that there were others who died in Perpignan because of her actions and so I decided to find out exactly what it was she meant. After much searching I located this in a box that had been lost amongst others in the record room.'

'Lost?'

'Discarded, I think. Unsolved deaths. Cases closed to further enquiry.'

'But their deaths were not my fault?' The room felt farther away than it had been and a spinning lightness consumed Cassie as she groped for the chair at her side and sat down upon it. Hard. Nathaniel perched before her, taking her hands in his own.

'This is the best wedding present anyone

could give us, Hawk,' he said, fingers warming
her coldness. 'Cassandra was already pregnant
when Guy Lebansart caught us at Perpignan.
By reciting the names she had seen on the letters in the place she had been captured, she
was trying to save both me and our baby.'

'But her confession and your injury took
place the day after the Desrosiers died and at
least a hundred miles to the south, so any information she gave was useless.'

'I didn't kill them.' Tears of deliverance fell
down her cheeks. 'I didn't,' she repeated, the
beauty of what the words implied washing
across her like a balm.

'You have both been to hell and back on
a lie. But you married her again, Nat, even
knowing this?'

'When you love someone, you love them,
Hawk, and there would be no argument in the
world that would keep me from Cassandra. But
this…this allows us peace.'

Standing up, he faced Stephen Hawkhurst. 'I
should have tried to find out all that transpired
after that day, but I could not. I never wanted
to sift through the files and know the betrayal.'

'Yet you kept her name out of everything.

I am not certain, had it been me, that I could have done that. King, country, oaths and all.'

Nathaniel laughed. 'They are all nothing against love, my friend. Wait until you find it.'

Gathering the documents, Stephen replaced them in the book. 'If Shavvon knew I had removed these...' He left the rest unsaid. 'But if I have them back tonight he will never need to know anything of it. He sends you his best, by the way.'

Cassie looked up at her husband and wondered just exactly who this Shavvon was that they were speaking of.

'Our boss,' Nathaniel explained quietly. 'At the Service.'

'But now this case is closed. For good.' Stephen faced them both as he promised this and then he was gone, the documents in hand as the door closed behind him.

'A marriage and a reprieve,' Nat said as he drew Cassandra up against him. 'A binding and a freedom. It has been quite a day, Lady Lindsay.' She could feel his breath against her cheek, soft and known.

'Lady Lindsay. I like the sound of that.'

'My wife. An even better resonance.'

'And what of the marriage night?' she whispered, watching the flare of complicity and question in his pale eyes. 'I think we should celebrate Hawk's gift.'

'I am completely at your disposal, my beautiful *Sandrine*,' he returned, lifting her into his arms and taking her to bed.

Chapter Thirteen

The past week had been a whirlpool of activity. Maureen's delight at her news, her father's quiet pleasure at having three daughters now in advantageous unions and Jamie's thrilled disbelief that the papa he had so often spoken of was promising to buy him a horse when they arrived at St Auburn.

After their wedding Cassandra had been inundated with calling cards, every door into society now open to her, though Nathaniel seemed distracted by his own work with the Service. She confronted him about it late on the third night after their marriage when she had gone down to the library to find him surrounded by papers.

'You look busy.'

'Busy missing some clue that I am certain is right in front of me,' he returned and stood.

'It is the girls from the river and Sarah?'

He nodded. 'Have you ever heard of the name Scrivener Weeks?'

'No. He is the man who you think killed them?'

'I do. I went to Wallingford and discovered that a few months ago another young woman was murdered there. A tall, dark and well-dressed man signed into the tavern late on the night the body was found, using the name of Scrivener Weeks. He left on the London coach early the next morning. No one can truly remember what he looked like.'

'He could be anyone.'

'Not quite. I think he is a member of the Venus Club.'

'Like Uncle Reginald?' Another thought occurred. 'That is why you and Stephen Hawkhurst joined up in the first place?'

He smiled. 'It is easier to keep an eye on people at close quarters. For what it is worth I have discounted your uncle.'

'Why?'

'He was ill with some sort of a chest infection when the girls were found on the riverbank here in London. He has the same physician as Hawkhurst does and the doctor was adamant Reginald Northrup could not have left his sick bed for a fortnight.'

'How many members does the club have?'

'Sixty-eight, and I have a group of thirteen names who fit the description of Scrivener Weeks.'

'We leave for St Auburn tomorrow. Could Stephen Hawkhurst take over until we return?'

'He will. I have told him my thoughts and given him the names. Perhaps he will see something that I have not.'

'Sarah would be thankful to you for your time and effort in finding her killer.'

'I haven't yet.'

'But you will.'

At that she took his hand and led him upstairs.

Late the next afternoon Cassandra could barely believe that they were almost at the principal country seat of the Lindsays, the fields about them rolling and green.

'Will we be there soon, Papa?'

She smiled. Jamie never spoke to Nathaniel without adding on 'Papa'. He had lost four years of his father and now he was making up for it. Sitting on Nathaniel's knee, he looked at the various landmarks that were pointed out.

'I used to swim in that river when I was very young. My father made wooden boats and we would sail them in the summer. Often they got stuck so I would jump in to rescue them.'

'Can you make me a boat, Papa? We could do that, too.'

Cassandra's heart swelled as her husband looked over at her, kissing the top of Jamie's head as he did so. Maureen, Kenyon, Rodney and her father would be arriving the day after tomorrow and she was pleased to have a couple of days to settle in. The only cloud on the horizon was Nathaniel's grandfather for they had not heard a word from him.

'The first sight of the house can be seen past this rise,' Nathaniel said and lifted Jamie higher. Cassie leaned forward to see it, too, and an enormous Georgian mansion materialised out of the distance, the six pillars across the front edifice flanked by two plainer wings, sitting on a hill. The tree-lined driveway wound towards it, a lake of grand proportions to one side.

'St Auburn is beautiful.' She could not keep the worry from her words.

'And big,' Jamie added.

'It's home,' Nathaniel said and reached for her hand. 'Our home.'

He had placed three of his staff into running the ledgers for the Daughters of the Poor and with his sizeable cash donation Cassie knew that all the work she had done would be left in competent hands. She would still hold regular meetings with Elizabeth and the staff, but the night-time rambles had ended and part of her was glad. This was a new chapter of her life and one she relished.

A line of servants had come out to greet them and there at the front door was an elderly man who Cassie reasoned would be Nathaniel's grandfather. He leaned upon a stick and watched them carefully as the conveyance drew to a halt.

Jamie was out first, the sun on his hair mirroring his father's and a sense of urgency and life on show that he had inherited as well. He looked right at home here, the tall yellow walls behind him with their meticulously pointed stone and inset windows. No small task for the masons, this building would have taken years and years to construct.

The old man came forward, his face devoid of expression. 'You have come back,' he said.

'We have come home,' Jamie cried. 'This is going to be my home now with the lake and boats.'

'Indeed?'

Such curling indifference had the effect of bringing Jamie closer to Nathaniel, fingers entwined in the expensive superfine of his father's trousers.

'William, this is my wife, Cassandra, and my son, Jamie.'

Pale silvered eyes whisked across her, calculating and assessing, and then they travelled over Jamie, the first glimmer of emotion showing.

'Well, at least he looks like a St Auburn. Does he like horses?'

'I have not ever ridden one, sir.'

'Grandpa,' he corrected. 'Call me Grandpa. Your father used to.'

A rebuke coined within the softness of memory. Nathaniel's hand tightened about her own, and Cassie hoped that whatever had gone wrong between them might soon be resolved.

After being introduced to the housekeeper and butler they walked along the line of other lesser servants, each one in a crisp and spotless uniform and all with generous welcomes. Once inside the Lindsay patriarch gestured for them to join him in a salon that ran along the front of the house, a room decorated in blues and greens.

'I was surprised that you finally realised St Auburn to be a duty you could encompass in your busy life, Nathaniel. Have you had enough of lying around in foreign taverns?'

Her husband's languid smile did not quite reflect his words. 'Protecting England from its enemies requires more than a nominal effort, William, though I do admit to a few drinks.'

Strong brandy to quell the pain of a gunshot wound in his side, but only water a few hours later as she had tried to clean it.

She wanted to say this to an old man who had much to thank his grandson for. She wanted him to see the hero in Nathaniel that she so often saw, a spy who had spent years undercover and in places that had hardly been kind. But she did not say any of this because she had no idea as to whether her husband would thank her for it or not. So she stayed quiet.

'The rooms on the first floor have been made up for you. Dinner will be at eight.'

With that he simply got up and walked away, the tap of his stick on the polished tiles becoming fainter and fainter.

'My grandfather has never been a man to show his feelings. This attitude, I suppose, was the reason my father and mother left here when I was young. They probably got the same sort of welcome we just did.'

'Does he not like us, Papa? Is he angry we are here?'

'No, he loves you, Jamie, but he is old and has gone to his quarters to have a rest.' Pulling his son up into his arms, he turned towards Cassie. 'Shall I show you to our room, my lady?'

'Certainly, my lord.' Suddenly all the politics of family squabbles did not matter at all. Tonight they would be together in a home that was theirs for good. She couldn't wait for the evening to come.

The chamber Nathaniel led them to was beautiful, with wide French doors leading out to a substantial balcony, pots festooned with greenery and flowers. Like in France, she thought, and looked across at the view. It was majestic. The far-off hills. The lake. The trees. The farm fields that went on and on for ever.

Jamie's room was a little farther down the corridor, flanked by the smaller nanny's quarters and a maid's room. To one side of Jamie's bed a whole row of old wooden toys were arranged on low shelves.

'They were once my father's. William must have instructed the servants to bring them down from the attic.' Nathaniel looked surprised.

'Did you play with them, too?' she asked as Jamie bent to draw a wooden train along the parquet flooring.

'I did. My grandfather was never very keen on the idea, though, for he thought I might break them. Perhaps he trusts you more, Jamie.'

'I will be very careful, Papa.'

'I know you will.'

Nat thought that the smile on Cassandra's face looked tightly drawn. She was obviously shocked by his grandfather's behaviour and by St Auburn, too. Most people on first seeing the place had the same sort of disbelief, but it was one of those houses that had grown over generations and there had always been plenty of money in the coffers of the Lindsays.

Plenty of money and not a lot of love. William had seen to that. He would get Cassie and Jamie settled and then he would go and find his grandfather. It was one thing for William to be rude to him, but quite another to be contrary with his wife and son. He would simply not put up with it.

But other things began to play on his mind, too. The way the sun slanted in upon Cassie's hair and the beauty of her face in profile. Crossing the room, he brought her close.

'Thank you for coming here with me. I am not sure if I would want to face it alone.'

'I think he is sad, your grandfather. How old were your parents when they died?'

'Thirty-four and twenty-eight.'

'Young, then. Imagine what that must have been like. Did he have a wife?'

'No. Margaret Lindsay died after my father left St Auburn.'

'Two terrible losses. And then the loss of you, as well, to the British Service and the further worry of the only family left to him never coming home.'

He smiled into her hair. 'I was about to go and growl at him. Now I am not so certain I should.' Nat had seen William's lack of feeling in terms of his own grief when he had lost his parents, but with Cassie's words a different understanding dawned. Imagine if he were to lose both her and Jamie. Would he still be able to function? He doubted it. Across her shoulders his son played with his new toys and beyond that again through the window the great lands of St Auburn spread out before him.

Home.

Here.

In Cassandra's arms, the scent of violets and woman and the promise of the passionate hours of night not far off.

'If this doesn't work we don't have to stay. There are plenty of other Lindsay properties.'

'But there is only one great-grandfather, Nathaniel, and Jamie needs to know him.'

Dinner that evening was a myriad of different emotions: William's distance, Cassandra's wariness and Nathaniel's equanimity. The room itself was beautiful with its carved table and tapestried chairs. On the wall around them were paintings from ground to ceiling displaying the images of relatives long dead. Their facial expressions looked about as happy as William's did as he sat at one end of the table.

'It is strange that you did not bring your family up to meet me sooner, Nathaniel.'

'We were married in France almost five years ago, but lost one another soon after. We resaid our vows a week ago.'

That brought a light to the old Earl's eyes and for the first time that evening a gleam of interest showed.

'There was a battle and a misunderstanding. I thought Cassandra had perished and she thought that I had, too. We met again only a handful of weeks ago by chance.'

'So you did not know your son?"

'I didn't.'

'He looks exactly as you did when you were that age. I should have some likenesses that were drawn at the time somewhere if you want to see them.' This was addressed at her.

'I should love to, my lord.'

'I will have them found tomorrow. There are other things, too, that I remember, a swing and a slide and a small rocking horse. Did he enjoy the toys in his room?'

Nat cleared his throat. 'He did. Thank you for thinking of it.'

'The boy and his mother can come with me on the morrow and we will go exploring for the rest of the toys that you and your father used to play with.'

A generous allowance and the first step into a truce from the battle of wits that Nathaniel and his grandfather seemed to be playing. Cassandra hoped that there would be many more across the next few days and weeks.

Much later Nathaniel and Cassandra lay in bed, holding each other and listening to the sound of a large house settling for the night: a clock in a distant hallway ringing out the lateness, the last swish of a maid's skirt as she went by on the final errands of the evening and a log in the fire shifting into a quieter burn. Jamie was fast asleep in his room. Nathaniel had tucked him in, all the love and concern of a father who wanted to savour the small moments he had so far missed in his care.

An hour earlier Nat had lifted her up in his arms, too, and placed her on his bed, positioning the frothy nothingness of her lacy night-gown just so.

'You cannot know how much I have longed for this moment, Cassie. To see you here at St Auburn as my wife.' He clasped her hand and turned the wedding ring that he'd had resized in London. 'We have done everything so far all the wrong way around. But from now on I mean to get it right.'

She shook her head. 'You have, my darling, all the way through. Ever since you first found me and took me out of Nay with a bullet hole in your side.'

Standing naked in the half-light of the fire, he looked like a large, strong panther, circling for all that she might give him, muscles shadowed and harsh. The tattoo stood out as did the white scars of battle. Her knight. Her hero.

Opening her arms, she brought him against her. This was the bed and the room that they would live in together for all the rest of their lives. When tears welled in her eyes and spilled down her cheeks, he pulled back in question.

'It is happiness, Nathaniel, only that.'

His forefinger came up to gently wipe away the moisture. 'I will love you for ever, Cassandra Sandrine Mercier Northrup.' The troth was given with a solemn honesty before his mouth closed down on hers.

The belltower attic was a place of wonder, a high-beamed room of generous proportion and a thousand forgotten things in it. With a new morning the old Earl seemed more fleet footed despite needing to manoeuvre around rolls of material and piles of papers. The toys were stacked on large, low shelves, numerous versions of balls and trains and soldiers and forts. One look at Jamie's face told her that they might be here a while.

'I like the big train best, Grandpa.'

The word *grandpa* seemed to sink into the deep lines of his face and flatten them out. 'I think if I look there are tracks for it somewhere.'

Cassie glanced around. 'I am sure Jamie feels as if all his Christmas days have come at once.'

'I think he may deserve it. Three years without a father is a long time.'

'Almost four,' she said quietly. 'His birthday is soon.'

They were interrupted by a squeal of delight. 'Look, Grandpa, look what it can do.'

He pulled the string behind the head of a large wooden puppet and the garish mouth opened to reveal a full set of yellowing teeth.

'That used to be my favourite, too,' William replied, bringing a large white kerchief from his pocket to dab at his eyes. As Jamie continued to explore, William started to speak of the past. 'Nathaniel is very like his father was, and forgiveness is not an easily won thing. When Geoffrey died, a part of me did, too, and I lost the little piece of him that I still had left in Nathaniel. Now it might be too late to find each other again.'

Cassie shook her head. 'Family should always be forgiven no matter what happens between them, for blood is thicker than insult or misconception. It only takes honesty.'

He smiled. 'My grandson was indeed lucky to find you.'

'He rescued me from a desperate situation and he did not judge me as he could so easily have done. His job there in France was a hard and dangerous one and if he hadn't come when he did...' She stopped, the horror of what might have been evident. 'England is fortunate to have someone like your grandson protecting its interests, and you should be proud that he carries your family name with such honour. I know I am.'

'I should have known, of course, for Geoffrey was a good man, too. It was just after my wife passed on that I felt so marooned and lost, and in my sorrow the happiness of my son's family gave me no relief. I pushed them away and never got them back.'

'Nathaniel did not come here to St Auburn again?'

'Oh, indeed, he did for a time after his parents died but by then we were set in our distance from each other and we barely talked. Later he wanted to modernise the place and I was determined to leave things as they were. After a while he hardly ever came home.'

'Well, we are here to stay now, and you will have all the chance in the world to talk with him. If you told him what you have just told me...'

She stopped as he nodded his head, and Jamie came up to him with a small boat complete with sails and ropes in his hands.

'Papa spoke about this in the carriage.'

'He did?' William took the craft and turned it this way and that. 'Your father's father made this, Jamie. If you bring it down we might be able to have a try at sailing the craft on the lake.'

'I will jump in and rescue it if it gets stuck, Grandpa.'

'Then we certainly have a deal.'

Maureen, Kenyon, Rodney and Lord Cowper arrived in the middle of the following morning, her uncle Reginald and his friend Christopher Hanley unexpectedly behind them in another conveyance. Nathaniel looked less than happy with the new arrivals as she glanced up at him. Something seemed wrong.

'I saw your father in London yesterday,' Reginald explained when the carriage stopped, 'and told him of my plans to head to the coast. When he asked if I would like to call in here at St Auburn for an hour or two, I was most grateful. I hope having Hanley here, too, will not upset anyone.'

The old earl looked about as pleased as Nathaniel did, and the arrival of Stephen Hawkhurst seemed to heighten the awkwardness yet again. Cassandra did not fail to see the look that went between her husband and his friend as they turned inside, and the

tension seemed to emanate from the presence
of Christopher Hanley.

Christopher Hanley sought her out an hour
later as drinks and a light repast were being
served in the front salon.

'You will not be so involved with your charity from now on, I suppose, Lady Lindsay?
Being here should take up much of your time.'

'No, in that you are wrong. I shall be as busy
with it as I ever was, and London is not far.'

'Was there ever any sign of Sarah Milgrew
and her sister's killer?'

'No, nothing, though we are still hopeful of
finding some clue to help us.'

'Your father continues to fund the Daughters of the Poor, then?'

'Indeed he does, and Nathaniel is involved,
too. My husband has brought Stephen Hawkhurst in for added assistance.'

Hawk watched them now, Cassie saw, his
eyes devouring Hanley's stance and face and a
small worm of uneasiness turned in her stomach. Something wasn't right, but she could not
quite put her finger upon it. She was pleased
when her uncle came to claim his friend in
conversation, allowing her to move away.

'You look worried.' William had joined her over by the windows. 'I knew Hanley's parents and they were not a happy couple. The father had a way with women of the night and the mother ran off with an Italian merchant and never returned to England.'

'A difficult upbringing for him, then?' Nathaniel had heard the last of the conversation as he came up behind her.

'You have had dealings with him?' William sounded interested in his grandson's answer.

'He has the unfortunate habit of poking his nose in other people's business. Suffice it to say he did Cassandra and me a favour in Whitechapel, but it could have been different.'

Uncle Reginald seemed to be making much of conversing with her father and for the first time in months Papa appeared happy. She supposed she should overlook the presence of the others here for an hour or two for it was good to see Papa smiling.

When Kenyon asked Nathaniel for a tour of the grounds of St Auburn everyone decided to go with them. Outside the sky was blue and the sun warm, and having partaken of food and drink a small exercise was desirable. Cassie was interested to see how Nathaniel shepherded Hanley, in particular, out through the front door.

Jamie was fractious though with all the excitement and so Cassie decided to stay back with him. A rest might see him through the afternoon pursuits and then he could have an early bedtime.

Bedtime.

She wished it were later already and that the hour to retire was here. Catching Nathaniel's eyes, she saw he watched her mount the stairs and she blushed with the warmth of his observance. Would there ever be a time when she could stand on the other side of a room fully dressed and in the company of others and not feel…desperate for him? She hoped not.

William, too, had decided to stay indoors because he found the heat oppressive. Concern marred Cassie's happiness. She prayed he would stay well and healthy enough to be a part of their family celebrations and outings for many years to come. They had only just found him again, after all, and underneath the gruff exterior was a man with a soft heart.

Half an hour later, sitting next to her sleeping son and thinking about her day, a new thought surfaced. Christopher Hanley had mentioned something about Sarah Milgrew, and Cassie sought to remember his words exactly.

He had asked about Sarah and her sister's killer. She sat forward, trying to pinpoint her uneasiness. The sister? Horror filled her. How had he known anything about Sarah's sister? The police themselves had not mentioned this and there had never been an identification carried out on the bodies of the earlier victims.

Oh, granted, Sarah had spoken of her sister's disappearance and Nathaniel had been interested in the gown of one of the drowned girls, but there had been no other information offered. Besides, the note that had arrived for Sarah the day she had disappeared alluded to information about knowing the whereabouts of her sibling, not the demise of her.

'My God.'

Standing, she indicated to a maid outside in the corridor to come in and sit with Jamie. Christopher Hanley was the tall, dark and well-dressed man. She was suddenly sure of it. He had been in Brown Street off Whitechapel Road when Nathaniel and she had found the body in the brothel, and the toff seen at the St Katharine Docks matched his description exactly.

Peering out the window on the stairwell, she noticed the group with Nathaniel to be perusing the formal gardens, but she could not see Christopher Hanley with them.

Fright made her heart beat faster as she hurried towards the front door. She had to get to Nathaniel to tell him what she suspected.

She had almost come into the wide hallway when a voice stopped her.

'I had a feeling I should return.' The sound came from behind and with all the effort in the world Cassandra made herself turn. She barely recognised the urbane and civilised lord, a sneer on his face and cold outrage in his eyes. Fear congealed in her throat and she could not hide her fright. 'I made a mistake talking to you earlier and I can see that you picked up on it.' Hanley's voice lacked any remorse whatsoever.

'You killed Sarah Milgrew and her sister. Why?' An explanation might buy her some moments for surely Nathaniel would be returning soon.

'They knew who I was. I thought after the first one I was safe and then the second girl turned up. I had killed their cousin in Wall-ingford, you see, and they remembered me.'

'And the man who was found dead at Brown Street?'

'Had come to London at the behest of their father to ask around and find out what had happened to the older sister. I couldn't let him ruin things.'

'So you tried to ruin me instead. It was you who sent the note asking me to come to the boarding house.'

'A miscalculation, I was to think later, for I did not realise that you knew Lindsay so well. Without him there, I might have succeeded. When he visited me in London the other day I knew by his questions that he suspected some-thing.'

'Yet you still came to St Auburn?'

'To find out the lay of the land, Lady Lind-say.'

At that he moved forward and simply twisted her arm hard up behind her back. 'If you shout out, I will go straight up to your son's room and break his neck, do you under-stand? Like a chicken in a hen house. You or him. Make your choice.'

Fear ripped resistance into pieces. Cassie

would wait till they were outside before trying to flee. Nodding, she went with him, past the first door and then the second, no servant in sight, the coast clear for his escape.

The third door was different. William Lindsay, the old Earl of St Auburn, was waiting in all readiness and with a shout he raised his cane and brought it down hard upon Hanley's head before falling.

The ungainly upending might have saved all their lives, she was to think later, for William took a sideboard full of bottles and glasses down with him and the noise was enough to wake up the dead. Blood dripped down into his closed eyes and Cassandra was certain that he had broken every bone in his body.

Hanley did not waver, finding an open window in the next salon and pushing her through it headfirst where she landed heavily onto an uneven brick wall and lost her breath.

'With you out of the way my secret will be safe and a quick escape to France will see to my own future.'

Shock had made him shake, and she felt his wrath course through her as he dragged her into the bushes surrounding the lake. Without hesitation, he pushed her into the water.

Icy coldness settled quickly.

Then his hands were about her throat, squeezing and squeezing. She tried to fight, she did, tried to stop him as the green of the water closed over her head, but already the world had begun to narrow into darkness. Sharp rocks dug into her back.

Floating. Peacefulness. The last release of bubbles as the warmth of death became brighter.

Then there was a noise, a hard punch and scream and a further whip of knuckles. The grip about her throat released and Cassie was lifted gently from the cold to be brought up into the arms of her husband where he cradled her against his warmth.

'It is all right, my love. You are safe.'

She was coughing, long, deep gasps of coughing, the air hard to find and the cold making it harder again. Her throat ached and her back had been bruised as Hanley had forced her down, but she was alive.

Alive.

Then she was crying, huge throaty sobs, her hands entwined in the fabric of his jacket.

'Your…gr-gr-grandfather tr-tried to s-save me.'

'I know, sweetheart. Don't try to talk just

now. I will take you back to the house and a bath will be drawn.'

A bath. Warmth. She gritted her teeth together to try to stop the dreadful shaking and felt the heat from his skin beneath her cheek.

Nat lifted Cassie, making certain that he averted his gaze from the dark red bruises that were gouged into her throat and from the cut beneath her eye. If Hanley had not been unconscious, he would have hit him yet again. Her hair was tangled with weed from the lake, the mud at the bottom smeared across her face and shoulders.

So damn close.

Another moment and they could not have saved her. He looked over at his grandfather, worse for wear from his upending, and saw the same thoughts in the opaque eyes. With a smile, he bent his head. In homage and in gratitude. Without William's quick-thinking actions…?

He shook away the horror.

Cassie was still crying, but her sobs were softer now. Her breathing had eased a little, too, and the pale white of her skin was rosier.

Her colour was returning and her fright receding. He was glad Kenyon was there to help his grandfather walk, the back of his head already showing signs of a bruised swelling. Maureen had taken his other side and she was speaking to him in the quiet and restful tones of one who seldom panicked.

A family that would be there for each other when the times got tough. A group of people joined by blood and love. He kissed his wife's cold forehead as he strode up the steps of St Auburn and the startled servants came running.

He found his grandfather in the library an hour later, sitting and looking out of the window with a heavy bandage around his head.

'William.' Today the word did not sit upon his tongue with the ease that it always had. 'Grandfather,' he amended and saw the old man turn.

'Is your wife recovered?'

'She is having a hot bath. The maids are with her and the warmth will stop the chills.'

'And Hanley?'

'Hawk has taken him back to London where he will be dealt with.'

'I would kill him if it were left to me.'

The sentiment made Nat smile. 'In that we are alike.'

'Are we?'

This time Nathaniel knew it was something else entirely of which William spoke. 'You never wanted my mother and father anywhere near you. You sent them from St Auburn and refused to ever see them again.'

'My Margaret had just died. I was not thinking straight and afterwards...' He hesitated. 'Afterwards it was too late. But now I see what I have missed.'

'You saved Cassandra. Without your bravery Hanley might have drowned her without a whisper.'

The earl shook his head. 'I hit him as hard as I could and it barely touched him.'

'But the noise when you fell alerted us. I owe you everything.'

His grandfather used his cane and came to stand next to Nat. 'We are both hard-headed and stubborn, Nathaniel, and we both love our wives with all our hearts.' The old eyes were watery as he placed his hand forward palm up. 'And our children.'

Pleading lay in the gesture. For family, it said, and for forgiveness, it asked.

Stepping forward, Nat brought his grandfather into his arms, tightly wrapped in an emotion that he had thought would be impossible.

'Thank you for saving her, Grandfather.'

'It was my pleasure, Nathaniel. And thank you, too, for saving me.'

Chapter Fourteen

She was wrapped in the warmth of wool and settled onto the generous blue sofa in the downstairs parlour.

Cassandra had had her hair washed and her body powdered and her feet were swathed in slippers of the finest lambswool, a present from William and one he had bought for his wife just before she had died.

She felt blessed. Jamie was cuddled into her side, and Nathaniel sat on a leather chair only a few feet away.

'If you had not been there, Grandfather, this could have all turned out far differently.' Her husband's words held a reverence and respect that was heartwarming.

'Which just goes to show that there is life in the old boy yet.' She saw William's hand rest lightly on Nathaniel's shoulder. They had spoken privately, she knew, before coming downstairs and the feud that had parted them seemed all but gone.

Reginald also had turned out to be a surprise. He had offered Cassandra a more than generous amount to be put into the coffers of the Daughters of the Poor plus the free use of a property that he owned in Aldwych as a place to set up further employment. Compensation for his poor choice of friends, he had told everyone. He had also decided to leave the Venus Club.

When Cassie glanced over at Nathaniel she saw that he was watching her closely.

'Good things come out of bad,' he said and smiled, though when his eyes settled on the marks at her throat an edge of anger was still visible.

Protection. It was so very relaxing. She closed her eyes and slept.

Much later when she awoke she found that she was back in their own chamber, but Nathaniel was not in bed with her. He stood at the window, looking over the land of the Lindsays, a moon hanging in the sky. The calmness that was so much a part of him made her smile and she simply watched.

'You cannot sleep, Nathaniel?'

The effects of the toddy the housekeeper had made for her had almost worn off now, and Cassie felt as if the shadows and mirrors she had lived with all her life had been thrown away somehow, the strong lines of hope exposed by love instead.

'I could not live if you left me, Sandrine. I could not find a way to keep on going. Today when I thought...' His voice broke, and he turned away, but not before she saw the moisture on his cheeks and the terror in his eyes. 'I never slept with another woman after Perpignan. It has always been just you.'

Pushing back the covers, she joined him at the window, winding her arms about his coldness and infusing warmth.

'Love holds no barriers, my darling. Time. Distance. Space. They are just words against love. We will always be together because we will always love.'

'Do you promise?'

'Come to bed and I will show you how I know,' she whispered, the heat of ardour rising. 'Let me take you to a place that is only ours.'

'Like the memory of the high baths above
Bagnères-de-Bigorre?'

She nodded and, taking his arm, led him
back to the warm nest of their bed.

As often thro' the purple night,
Below the starry clusters bright,
Some bearded meteor trailing light,
Moves over still Shalott.

* * * * *

A sneaky peek at next month…

HISTORICAL

AWAKEN THE ROMANCE OF THE PAST…

My wish list for next month's titles…

In stores from 4th July 2014:

- ☐ A Lady of Notoriety – Diane Gaston
- ☐ The Scarlet Gown – Sarah Mallory
- ☐ Safe in the Earl's Arms – Liz Tyner
- ☐ Betrayed, Betrothed and Bedded – Juliet Landon
- ☐ Castle of the Wolf – Margaret Moore
- ☐ Rebel Outlaw – Carol Arens

Available at WHSmith, Tesco, Asda, Eason, Amazon and Apple

Just can't wait?

0614/0

Special Offers

Every month we put together collections and longer reads written by your favourite authors.

Here are some of next month's highlights— and don't miss our fabulous discount online!

On sale 20th June

On sale 4th July

On sale 4th July

 *Save 20%*
on all Special Releases

Find out more at
www.millsandboon.co.uk/specialreleases

Join our *EXCLUSIVE* eBook club

FROM JUST £1.99 A MONTH!

Never miss a book again with our hassle-free eBook subscription.

★ Pick how many titles you want from each series with our flexible subscription

★ Your titles are delivered to your device on the first of every month

★ Zero risk, zero obligation!

There really is nothing standing in the way of you and your favourite books!

Start your eBook subscription today at www.millsandboon.co.uk/subscribe

 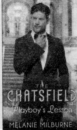  

BP 6.14

Join the Mills & Boon Book Club

Want to read more **Historical** books?
We're offering you **2 more** absolutely **FREE!**

We'll also treat you to these fabulous extras:

- 🌹 **Exclusive offers and much more!**
- 🌹 **FREE home delivery**
- 🌹 **FREE books and gifts with our special rewards scheme**

Get your free books now!

visit www.millsandboon.co.uk/bookclub
or call Customer Relations on 020 8288 2888

SUBS/ONLINE/H1